Biker Leather & Woolly Sheep

Fanny Garstang

Second Edition published 2022
First Edition published 2017

Cover Design by Judy Bellingham
Text Copyright © 2017 Fanny Garstang
All Rights Reserved

ISBN: 978-1-7396895-0-6

This is for my grandparents, Jean & Phil Griffiths, who have read every book- the good, the bad and the ugly, and never discouraged me.

.

1

The farm stood in a green valley. High hills circled it and looked down on the isolated farmstead. Their rocky slopes could only really support sheep, which could be seen roaming around the fields and gentler slopes. A stream ran past the garden and overgrown vegetable and fruit patch.

The main farm was not far away from the stream, but far enough to be safe from the flooding of the stream. The long house had a slate roof and faced out on to the courtyard, which sloped gently downwards. It had stood there for over century as farmhouse and labourer's cottage although at some point a door was knocked through the two. The only connections it had with the real world were electricity, the telephone and water.

A large barn took up the right-hand side of the cobbled courtyard with a modern pen attached to it. The left side contained a multitude of other outhouse buildings including an open fronted cart shed. Opposite the house, set into the hillside was a row of four stables of which only one was occupied.

Mist hung over the hills on this particular day. The rain streamed down from the heavens and down the courtyard. A young woman, in her late twenties stood leaning with her back against the gate looking down at the farm she had just bought with the winnings of her Millionaire Raffle entry.

Lily Harrison wore a woolly jumper over a shirt under her coat. As well as that she wore a pair of jeans and a pair of wellies on her feet. Her brown hair was pulled up into a ponytail to hide the fact she hadn't had a haircut since she'd left London a month ago. Her nails were just as bad and were in need of a manicure.

Having now been in the depths of Wales for the last month she was starting to wonder whether she had done the right thing. She had had her parents support, sort of. Her boyfriend had been whole-heartedly against it, claiming she was insane to want to leave London. She had thought it all quaint at the time and liked the idea of being her own woman and making a fortune out of organic sheep cheese or lamb with a B&B on the side. To be honest she hadn't completely thought it all through properly especially once she had stepped into the farmhouse for the first time. She had not just bought the farm but all its contents; furnishings, animals and all but it was the only farm she could afford.

She may own the farm and its land but she also had a business bank loan organised by her boyfriend on a low interest. On arriving she had realised she barely knew anything at all about farming, let alone sheep farming in the Welsh hills and had had to look for someone to be her farm manager. It was all too late to back out now. All she could do was hope that her boyfriend, Mac, might turn up to say hello but he had pulled the most appalling face when she had said where she was going. She knew that he, in his suits, would never enjoy the mud and rain. One look and he would probably develop hives, but there again, he might actually enjoy it. All she could do was wait and see as he was coming up in a few weekends time.

Hearing the sound of an engine and tyres on the gravel track she turned and spoke out loud to make her feel less alone, "it must be him."
Lily clambered over the wet gate and ran around the corner. She saw a van up ahead, at the top of the track. She stood in the middle of the track waving her arms around, grabbing the driver's attention. The van slowly drove down the track. The wheels left ruts in the mud as it slowly made its way down.

It stopped in front of her as she opened the two sides of the gate. She glanced up as the van went by and saw it was a woman at the wheel with two collies bouncing on the passenger side, one black and white and one brown and white. The van stopped in the courtyard as she walked down. The woman behind the wheel climbed out of the van with the two collies spilling out from behind her; and came forward in a pair of jeans and shirt with her black hair pulled back in a plait which was beginning to fall out of the rubber band. She asked, "Are you Lily Harrison?" "Yes." Lily replied cautiously.

"Sorry, obviously George didn't bother to let you know. I'm his sister, May, May Risoll. I'm just bringing his stuff over for him. He's somewhere back up the lane." "What are their names?" Lily asked as she tried to keep them from leaping all over her.

"Oh, sorry." The young woman grabbed the two collies by the collars while at the same time shouting. "Down Stan, down Lou. Sorry, they get excited with new faces. Don't worry, they'll calm down soon, hopefully. George has more control over them. Oh, by the way, I'm not staying. Just unloading his stuff for him, then I've got to get back to our farm."

"How much longer is he going to be?" Lily asked.

"Oh, depends on if he gets stuck behind anything on the road. Can I come in, get out of the rain?" The May answered bluntly.

"Err, of course. Sorry." Lily was taken aback by the girl's boldness as well as the thick Welsh accent.

They walked down the rest of the slippery cobbles to the front door of the farmhouse. Lily led her into the kitchen where the kitchen was just about unpacked from when she had arrived a month ago. Lily asked, "Do you want tea?"

"Please. I was lucky it wasn't snowing actually as if it snows we are normally trapped up this way." May remarked as she followed her through into the main room where the Aga was warming up the house and water. May leant against the Aga warming her fingers while Lily plonked a battered iron kettle on one of the hot plates. Lily cautiously asked, "how is George getting here then?" She was beginning to wonder if George was going to be as good looking considering how well his sister looked with her black hair and glowing skin from the country air though there was a hint of fragility about her as well.

"On his bike, he's got an old Triumph he did up. It helps him round up the sheep when the dogs are being a bit pathetic. I know this place." May cheerfully chatted on.

"You do?" Lily was surprised.

"Yeah, it was an old couple."

"I ended up with their two hairy ponies." Lily remarked.

"They weren't put down, that's good. There's said to be a ghost here. They had a big party for their golden anniversary. I haven't seen it though. It haunts the back stairs apparently; well that's what my ma said. Hey, can I see the ponies? I just want to be able to tell mum they are ok."

"Mmm, sure. Are there any tricks I need to know about them?" Lily enquired as they headed out of the house to the stables with their tea.

"Just check their hooves occasionally. George can do that though. We have a horse of our own."

They headed for the stables where the two sturdy welsh mountain ponies stood warm and dry. Their hooves made the straw rustle and a cloud of straw dust rose up. They snorted as they saw the two young women enter before settling down again. May patted them on their velvet noses, "there, there. If I can find a saddle that fits perhaps we can go for a ride. I haven't been out for ages."

May slowly moved away from them. The pair stared at her through their large brown eyes. She took a rough brush from a toolbox and began to brush them down till they began to shine in the dusty light of the stable. The rain continued to drum on the tiled roof of the stable.

Everything was peaceful and the rain was soothing. May felt relaxed in the quiet and only jumped at what sounded like thunder echoing around the valley. Instead of fading away the sound got louder making the two women look at each other. They looked at the ponies; they weren't frightened so it couldn't be thunder. May smiled, "it's him. You go meet him, just tell him I'm with the ponies."

"You sure?"

"Yeah. He'll know I'm here since the dogs are having a good sniff round and the van is parked in the courtyard."

Lily ran out into the rain where she could hear the noise more clearly. She was becoming curious about this man George. Once outside she realised it was definitely the sound of a motor. She ran up the yard passing the van and slipping on the cobbles. She reached the gate and stood on the other side of the open gate looking up the track.

A Triumph Bonneville motorbike came through the trees. The rain decided to stop and for a brief moment the sun came out and made the droplets of water on the tank of the black bike shine for once considering it was normally splattered with mud. The bike shone, but the tyres were caked in mud. On the seat of the motorcycle was a person clad in black. The bike skidded to a stop, spraying watery mud at Lily and the rider slammed the foot down. He climbed off the bike and stood facing her.

She took the newcomer in. He wore biker trousers speckled with mud and a classic style black leather jacket that made her think of James Dean. His hands were hidden by black gloves, which he was now removing. He put them on his bike and his hands went under his helmet. She heard a muffled click and the helmet came off the visitor's head. Lily gave a small gasp as she saw the man's head. The man tossed his head, shaking his black hair back into life, after being flattened by the ride, the curls bounced back into shape as well. His grey eyes were friendly. Both the hair and eyes were from his Italian great-grandfather who had been a prisoner of war who had stayed. Everything else about him was from his mother, who was Welsh through and through.

He put his helmet on the motorbike before introducing himself to Lily, "I'm George. Has May arrived yet with the two dogs?"

"Yes she did, I'm Lily." She responded shyly with a redness rising in her cheeks. His face transfixed her. He was quite handsome with his black hair matching the black leather he wore. George smiled at her; it was only a small one, moving one corner of his mouth. He had realised that she was feeling surprised by what he looked like, he didn't really worry about his appearance, but he knew that women were attracted to him.

She couldn't believe herself for turning all feeble and girlie on this man that she had just met but for her he was absolutely gorgeous; more than that, a god! He was a hell of a lot better looking than Mac back in London. Her mind started to wonder if she could get rid of her boyfriend and take George instead but she forced herself to stay on track. Mac was her banker boyfriend and George was her farmhand. He held out his left hand and undid the collar of his jacket with his right. She gingerly took and shook his hand.

Lily was stunned by his voice. It was a deep voice, which was alive with the singsong Welsh accent, though it was stupid to be surprised by the accent as they were in Wales. In the back of her mind she had vaguely been thinking that he was coming from England. He suggested, "Why don't you take me to May."

"Where do you want to put your bike?"

"A shed will do for it."

"Follow me." She turned and opened the gate to let George and his bike through. He handed his helmet over to her; it shone as much as the machine. He lifted up the foot and pushed the motorbike steadily forward. It rattled as it went over the cobbles, bouncing over them. The two reached the large cart shed which currently held an animal trailer and a mud splattered Land Rover. She pointed inside and said "You can put it in there."

"So you inherited his Land Rover as well." He chuckled. She smiled back nervously. Was there something she should know about it?

Apart from some horrendous gears it seemed to go alright.

If she were a weak person she would have fainted away by now she thought. She started to wonder if she was flirting with him, and hoped she wasn't. *Think Mac, think Mac,* she reminded herself.

He came back out and swept his hair back. He walked into the courtyard that fronted the house and looked around, "Which end am I living at then?"

"That end." Rosie pointed to the end of the house closest to them.

"The haunted end then. That's good, then I'll be able to tell May if the ghost really does exist, not that I believe in them myself. Do you? Hello boy." He smiled as Stan ran up to him and jumped up to lick his face. He gave the shaggy dog a rub round the dog's black mane, "Yes, this is your new home. Now, where's your girl? Lou?! Come here girl." The other collie appeared and leapt up at him, "ok, behave yourselves now. I just need to talk with our new boss.

"Go to May." He pointed down the courtyard and they bounded off to May in the stables while he followed Lily.

Entering the house he pulled his wet jacket off with the comment, "lord, it was wet out there, enough to fill the reservoirs twice over. I know I start tomorrow but thought it best to come a day early so I can settle in. I'll give the sheep a once over if I have time tonight but as they are the last of Mr Lewis' flock they should be in good nick. He took good care of them even if it meant he didn't live very well. You planning on get any more?"

"Umm, yeah, not that I really know. I had a vet up and he said they were all okay, possibly some pregnant by the ram Mr Lewis rented before he died." Lily remarked though she couldn't help but stare since George's t-shirt revealed well-tanned, muscular arms though the right wrist was paler than the other and had a few scars. It made her wonder what had happened to him recently. He drew a breath through his teeth, "Vets are expensive. It's best only to call them when they are really needed. I'll check Mr Lewis' bits and renew any tablets, powders and vials if they are a bit old."

"I was wondering what that shelf of bottles was for."

"What bits up the end are mine then?"

"At the moment you have a bathroom, bedroom and sitting room. You are down this end for the kitchen as there isn't one up there yet. Come with me and I'll show you."

"That sounds just fine to me, thank you. You don't have to show me. Do you have the key and me and May will get my bits move in?"

"Umm, yes. Let me remember where I've put it." Lily began rummaging through a drawer in the old cupboard in the kitchen. She couldn't wait for the builders to come in and put in the new kitchen, "do you want some help?"

"The more hands the merrier." George smiled, "Come on."

It had been a long day what with moving to a new place with the help of May and Lily as well as having discussed what he would be doing with a bewildered Lily. He came to realise she knew barely anything and wondered if she had really thought about it all before buying the farm.

He yawned as he poured the can of soup into one of his two saucepans and lit the camping stove he had borrowed off his parents. Maybe tomorrow night he would dare make a trip down to the proper kitchen. He had waved

May off with a promise to drop in at home when he had a moment to.

His two dogs now lay on their rug in front of the small fire he had lit in the stove in the fireplace. They limply wagged their tails as he stood in the doorway between the tiled room that may well have been a kitchen once but Mr Lewis had pulled everything out apart from an old humming fridge and then forgotten about doing anything to it; and sitting room and he smiled at them. He completely agreed with the idea that they were man's best friend for they were certainly his. Although excitable they were well trained in their task of herding sheep. He would try again at this year's national trials to win a prize.

With the soup finished he dumped bowl and spoon on an unpacked boxes of books and headed to bed. He stumbled on the steps briefly before feeling his way up them and finding the cold latch of his new bedroom with its sloping room and small window covered in ivy. He had already made a note to clear the ivy off the window before it caused it to crack. It could be romantic having the summer sun shining through as green but he was not in a romantic mood and at this time of year he wanted as much sunlight coming in as possible. For the moment the light bulb would have to do as he reached for the knobbly wall and flicked the switch.

George looked at his new bedroom and it felt odd to not actually be in the family home with the noise that came with it. The blankets on his double bed included a multicoloured quilt made by his mother, a reminder of home. He pulled off his clothes and slipped into bed.

Up the other end of the house, Lily was contemplating an early night with the last of the red wine she had been trying to resist so it would be there for a time when she desperately needed to drown her sorrow in alcohol. Staring at it from across the table she wondered what May had meant when as she left she had asked her to take care of him. It had been said with a concern that was more than just sisterly love. She wondered if he would fancy joining her for a drink. The last month had been quite lonely and would be nice to have some company. Maybe she should invite May over at some point for the girlie company. She seemed nice. Once the house was suitable she would get her London friends over.

2

It may have been drizzling in the low clouds but he was still glad to be out in the fields with their off white slush. Stan and Lou ran ahead of him, sniffing along the wall lines as George staggered behind them in his battered barbour jacket and old overalls, leaning on his straight crook. In his free hand he carried an old feed bucket with tools and antiseptic spray.

Reaching the top field he looked down at the farm terraced into the hillside. The sheep were hunkered down around their shelter in the field closest to the farm where another pen had been permanently set up. At the other end was a couple of bales he had hauled out of the barn. He knew the flock had been shrunk to the bare minimum by Mr Lewis in his last years. Tomorrow he would find out what Lily's plans for the place were.

He pulled his hat lower and threw a few fallen stones back on to the stone wall. Someone had made a clumsy attempt to repair it to stop the sheep getting over. He would have to come back when it was warmer and break it down to rebuild it. He walked on round and down.

Lily watched him from her bedroom window. She didn't know what to make of him. He had already been up when she had stirred. She had seen the beam of the torch as he had entered the stable to feed and water the ponies. She wondered what to make for their dinner. She felt sure he would want something more substantial then the beans on toast she had been living off along with cereal.

The problem was she was no cook. Back in London Mac more often then not took them out for dinner or ordered takeaway as his cooking skills were as bad as her own. She hoped George could cook but would it be fair to make him work all day with the animals and then cook them dinner. She had one cookbook and was sure she would find something easy in it to have a try at.

As he reached the field he whistled. Stan and Lou pricked their ears up and they bound up to him. He crouched down and in welsh said gently, "lets see how out of practice you are. This should be easy, it's only a small flock. Come by Stan and away Lou."
The two collies ran off in opposite directions as he pulled a dog whistle out of a pocket of his coat. With whistles and shouts and the occasional bit of swearing Stan and Lou managed to move the reluctant flock down into the pen.

Stan and Lou lay behind him as he closed the gate of the pen. He turned on them, "that was not a winning display."
They just panted with pricked up ears. George smiled at them as he climbed over the metal pen. He needed to reassure himself that they were all in good health and see how many of them were pregnant. With a spray can he marked any he thought were pregnant before letting them back out into the field.

With the last one back out in the field he leant against the pen fencing. That had been harder than usual. He flecked his healed wrist and decided he had done enough for the day considering he had been told to take it gently to begin with. Leaning more on this stick then he planned to he walked down to the farmyard with Stan and Lou behind him.

He walked into his cottage and pulled off all his wet and muddy clothes. It was past lunch but all he wanted was to warm his body with a lobster hot bath. He needed to speak to Lily but his body demanded warmth.

Lily brightened at the sight of George with his damp hair in a shirt, jumper and jeans. She put the lid back on the pot and smiled, "I was starting to think you had got lost. Cup of tea?"

"Please."

She had just made herself one so passed it over to him, "are your rooms ok?"

"They are fine thanks. Something smells good."

"I thought I'd try making something other then beans on toast. It's nearly done." She smiled shyly. Oh, he looked so good.

"That's all right then. I'm starving." He sat at the dining table, "so you have Mr Lewis' books."

"Mmm, yeah, they are here somewhere." She rummaged through the pule of paperwork she hadn't sorted and found the hard backed books, "here you go. What are you looking for?"

"From the ewes that are left about two thirds of them are pregnant. His books should give me a better idea of how many were ridden by the tup."

"Oh, I know that word now." She exclaimed as she sat down by his side as he opened the red book to the back pages, "how many am I going to need to make any money?"

"He used to have about a hundred. You'll have to build the flock up over a few years and find yourself a decent tup. He was always good with his records. This column," he pointed at the second column, "gives you the ear tag id number. Then it's sex and then birth date so we know how old it is followed by when it was sold and how much for. That's the easy one. This book," he reached for the blue book, "tells you which ewes got ridden by the tup and which one if he borrowed a few and then roughly when he had them. He'd sold most of his flock so he only had the one tup this time round. Mmm, yes, about right."

"What?" She peered over his arm to look at the page, "is something wrong?"

"No. My count and his are about the same. Um, what's that smell?" They both looked over to the aga as Lily exclaimed, "fuck!" She ran over and pulled the saucepan across, "it's ruined."

"Lets have a taste first." He said at her side. She felt her stomach tighten. He reached for the spatula and gave her chilli a taste. Lily watchied his face fearfully and her face fell as his twisted up. He remarked, "it may have smelt good but it sure doesn't taste good. What were you trying to make?"

"Chilli with rice?"

"And the rice is in this saucepan?" He pointed at the one waiting to go on the hotplate.

"Shoot!" She exclaimed.

"You haven't cooked on an aga before?"

"No." She blushed.

"And cooking?" She shook her head, "the best I can do is beans on toast." She admitted.

He laughed and then soberly asked, "should you really be here at all?" She frowned at him, "yes I should be. I'm going to prove to everyone that I can do it. This is what I've always wanted to do. I have plans for this place." He held his hands up in submission, "ok, ok. I submit." As he lowered them he added, "apart from beans and bread do you have anything else here? I really could do with something to eat."

"Be my guest." Her shoulders slumped as she gestured towards the kitchen. Why did she have to drink that wine last night? She could have done with it now to drown her sorrows over her terrible cooking.

"You really don't have much do you?" George remarked from the kitchen, "have you seen if your ducks and chickens are producing eggs yet?" Entering the kitchen she confessed, "no."

"I'll show you in the morning. Right beans on toast it is." He sighed with a laugh.

"I'll find us something to drink." She replied with a smile, "we'll go shopping tomorrow?"

"Sure. We are going to need more than beans and bread if we are going to be eating together."

With a flourish he produced two plates of beans on toast with a grin,

"beans on toast al a George."

"Cheese." Lily exclaimed with surprise, "why did I not think of that?"

"More than that. I found one lonely egg and some mustard and made rarebit." He put a plate in front of her as she poured the wine.

"So you didn't bother with much food but remembered the alcohol?" He teased, "you're a woman after May's heart."

"Tell me more about her, and you." She asked as they started to eat.

"She's my little sister and mad about horses."

"She can have the two ponies if she wants. I think the sheep are going to be bad enough."

"It's alright. It will give her an excuse to come over." She liked the idea of that.

"She's training to be a teacher which is great for her. She has only told me but she wants to escape and this is a way out for her." He added as he studied the glass of red wine.

"I'll help if I can. I've got friends in London."

"That would be great." He beamed at her.

She gulped. *Oh that smile. Stop it- you have Mac.* She reminded herself, "what about yourself? Why haven't you left?"

"I like it up here. I used to help Mr Lewis." He hesitated.

"Use to?"

"That's why I've been roped in to help you." He changed the subject, "and I've been trying to get into the sheepdog trial championships as well. Is that all right if I practice? Mr Lewis use to let me."

She finished her glass and filled it again, "sure."

"So?" He leant in, "what about yourself? How have you ended up here? What are your plans for the place?"

"I was thinking of going organic?" She glanced at him to see his reaction. He didn't say anything so she went on, "and sell the meat. I'll have a go with cheese as well. I've done a cheese making course so think I'll be able to do it. And then just to help me a long I'm going to use some of the bedrooms as a B&B. People like staying on farms right?"

He looked thoughtful, "well you have plenty to work on. Am I going to be getting a lot of practice fry ups?"

"Maybe, unless you volunteering?" She cheekily asked.

"I'm here for the animals. If you want to look after guests you'll have to learn to do cooked breakfasts."

"Fine."

"When is all this happening?"

"Next few months."

"If you want to have any chance of having enough milk for cheeses you are going to need a bigger flock."

"We can buy more?"

"Lets see what we get at lambing and go from there. We may get some males we can sell which then can be put towards some more ewes."

"Good idea."

He rolled his eyes. This job was certainly going to be interesting.

3

After an uneventful shopping trip and once the animals were fed and cleaned out George found himself being roped into decorating. Lily seemed to be determined to get the house presentable in time for Mac's visit in two weeks time. He also found himself turned into the housecook which Lily was relieved about. If he didn't watch out he would be cooking B&B breakfasts.

A builder was in redoing the main bathroom and kitchen as well as putting in a little en-suite to Lily's bedroom. He did point out he had no kitchen but she didn't seem to hear him. She had heard him but didn't have the money. She needed to get guests in from spring onwards to pay the bills

He was relieved when May gave him a call at the end of the week. He pushed Lou off the worn out sofa as he sat down, "it's good to hear a sane voice."

"Oh. Is is that bad?"

"Not sure. I seem to have been roped into decorating."

"Decorating? Have you not got much to do?"

"If I tried I probably could but sheep look after themselves as you know. None of them have tried to commit suicide yet. God knows how she'll react then."

"Decorating?"

"Yeah." He sighed, "she's got about three plans on the go. One of them is to open as a B&B."

"Oh. Can she cook then?"

He laughed, "no, unless you want beans on toast or cereal."

"Are you looking after yourself?"

"Found some new aches but I'm doing alright. You?"

"The same. It doesn't help I'm back on my hands and knees with reception." "Oh, Lily said she can help you if you want to go to London."

"Ssh." At the other end May glanced round the family farmhouse.

"When are you going to tell her?" He asked with a sigh.

"Well, I was until he…, well…. You know." It was still something they didn't really talk about. She could talk about it with her therapist but had yet to talk about it with anyone else, especially her brother. She didn't know how he was doing mentally as he didn't talk about it either. They skirted around it.

"Do you want to come over this weekend?" He asked after a moment of silence.

May brightened, "yes please. How are the dogs?"

"Out of practice."

"I'm not surprised. Mum was letting them lie in front of the range."

"Bring a sleeping bag and I'll take the sofa."

"I'll bring a sleeping bag but, I'll take the sofa." She replied sternly, "and I'll bring a bottle as well."

"You can share that with Lily then."

"As long as you have a glass as well. Oh, tell her that I may have found a saddle, I'll bring it with me." May said excitedly.

"Aren't they a bit old?"

"I'm sure Bertie can cope with a novice."

"Mmm. And what about Jinx? Have you been back on him yet?"

"I did for a little bit when I should have been writing up lesson plans." She admitted.

"And?"

"I was stiff afterwards but I did enjoy it. You should borrow one of Katherine's and join me."

"I'll think about it. What time should I expect you tomorrow?" He yawned. He didn't know what was more exhausting, the animals or decorating.

"After lunch. I'll get my homework out of the way."

"Alright. See you then."

"Take care till then."

"You know I will."

"I mean it." She said sternly with unspoken words behind it.

"Cheer up. You get to see me tomorrow and get jumped on by filthy dogs."

"Alright. Till tomorrow."

"Tomorrow." And he hung up on her before she could say another word.

He looked into the fire which Stan was slumped in front of, bumping the phone against his chin. He knew his sister still felt guilty about it all but he had chosen to interfere and he didn't regret it especially as the guy was now being held on two accounts of grievously bodily harm. They were just waiting for the case to go to court. But enough, they were both alive and that was the important bit and she was coming over tomorrow. He'd best spend an hour tidying otherwise she would be rolling her eyes at the mess.

He got up and shook the blanket covering the sofa on the floor. Dried mud fell to the floor and he sighed. He was going to have to find the hoover. It was a good thing Lily hadn't ventured up his end. It looked like a man's farmhouse. Mr Lewis would have been proud while Mrs Lewis would not have been.

Lou and Stan glanced up as he gathered a few mugs up and disappeared out the door and then flopped back down. They knew they were pretty much banned from Lily's nice clean end with their dirty paws and coats. They did get brushed but then the next day it would be back.

As he stepped into the sitting room he mumbled, "sorry."

Lily looked up from where she sat wrapped in a soft blanket in front of the stove. She had prettied up the fireplace with a large collection of candles which she was using to read by. Beside her was a glass of wine and he frowned at the sight. He felt she was beginning to rely on the glass. She smiled at him, "hiya. Joining me?"

"No. Just on the hunt for the hoover. May is coming over tomorrow."

"That's nice."

"Enjoy the rest of your evening."

"Enjoy your cleaning." She teased and then wondered whether that had been a bit forward of her as he briefly frowned.

"Thanks." Just for a moment he liked the idea of abandoning the cleaning and sitting next to her instead. There was a romantic feel to the air. He shook his head. She had clearly stated she had a boyfriend and with lots of money as well. Why would she be interested in what was basically a shepherd on minimum wage and two dogs? She was starting to grow on him considering how much time they were spending together decorating. A part of him wanted Spring to arrive so that he could get back outside.

Watching him pass through and then back with the hoover Lily felt disappointed that he hadn't stayed. It was just the company she wanted she tried to convince herself. She was still trying to work out why she was attracted to him. Was it his looks? His skills with his hands? The gentleness about him? Or the mystery? Or was if the obvious fact that he was the only company she had. She contemplated ringing Mac again but the last time she had only got his answer machine. What was he up to this friday night? She wanted him to ring back for some phone sex.

May bounced into her brother's cottage. She dropped her bags on the floor, "hello?!"

The dogs bound in barking and she remarked as she pushed them down, "well at least you two are here to welcome me." She looked up when she heard the door open, "oh, there you are."

"Hi sis. Don't take your boots off. We'll go for a walk." He remarked as he hugged her.

"What about all the decorating? Do I get to see your handiwork?" She teased. She needed to give him the letter from court but didn't want to ruin his mood and the day.

"No."

"Come on then. Let's see how bad these two are at herding. Have you signed up to any trials yet?" She took his hand and dragged him towards the door.

"Haven't got any internet yet. Can you have a look?" He asked as he pulled on his boots, coat and hat. The dogs bounced around at their feet, "hungry?" He threw May an apple as he bit into one himself

As they walked out into the fields she tucked a hand into his elbow, "you didn't say much on the phone. What's she really like?"

"Don't start matchmaking. It's not even worth thinking about for two reasons. One, she is my employer and two she has a rich boyfriend in London."

"Oh, oh well. It was worth a try." She laughed and leant into him.

"Mmm. Here we go. Let's see if we can get Stan and Lou to separate a few of the flock off."

They stood now in the field with the sheep.

He sent Stan and Lou off in opposite directions and with the whistle they crept in and then ran pass each other to separate five of the flock. With them separated he whistled and called them into a close pack flock and then herded them towards the shelter. George remarked, "and shut the gate. Yes. That wasn't bad." He turned to May and they high-fived, "what do you think?"

"Some tightening up could be done but I think they'll be all right. How many of them are pregnant?"

"About two thirds of them. Stan come over here. Stan!" Too late he had rolled in fox. George rolled his eyes, "you're getting the hose when we get back." Turning back to his sister he went on, "what I was about to say was I think it will be worth doing some training with them solo, just in case. Lou would be the better of the two."

"Definitely. What's for dinner chef?"

"Hungry already?"

"Oh yes. Paperwork can make you very hungry."

"All right. We'll see if Lily wants to join us otherwise she'll be having a bowl of cereal."

They made their way through the farmhouse where they found Lily muttering over the instructions of a bed frame while an I-pod played in the background. They stood in the door frame as Lily tried to work out what screws she needed. May asked, "need a hand?"

"Oh." Lily looked up with relief, anything for help or escape, "hello?"

"Hello. Want some help otherwise George was going to make dinner."

"Both please."

"You haven't done many flat packs have you?" May remarked as the siblings entered the room.

"No." Lily answered feeling sheepish

"Well, neither have I so that makes two of us." May cheerfully commented,
"you George?"

"I'm use to making do."

"I'm sure three heads can get this done." May picked up the instructions, "it can't be any worst then teaching little ones their numbers and alphabet."

It still took them an hour to do it but by the end May had them all laughing as with a teacher's voice she told them what to do. Lily hadn't had so much fun a while. Wait till she told her friends. They heaved the mattress on and then dropped on to it together. George remarked, "I'm glad that's over."

"There's another two to go plus some bedside tables and wardrobes." Lily corrected.

"No, no and no. I'll hide." He sat up.

"I'll take you down the pub for some dinner?"

"That sounds like a decent reward." May rolled on to her side.

"What's for dinner?" Lily rolled over as well.

"I'm feeling ganged up on. I think I'll be safer in the kitchen." He stood up and grimaced as he stretched before leaving the room. May spotted it but resisted asking. She turned to Lily, "have you got a corkscrew? I brought some wine with me and George isn't a big drinker."

"I've noticed. Is he a beer man?"

"Not really. Come on, I left it up the other end."
Shyly Lily remarked, "you've got really good nails."

"I can do yours while dinner is cooking if you want."
Lily looked down at her nails and then at May, "that would be nice." She had found May a bit in your face that first day but having spent the last hour in her happy company she quite liked her now. She came across so happy-go-lucky without a care in the world. She hadn't seen the slightly haunted look in the woman's eye whenever she looked at George. Maybe later they could talk about girlie things; the sort of stuff that normally drove men out of the room.

George hummed as he moved between the kitchen and the aga. The dogs were being allowed the rare treat of lying in front of the aga though Lily's nose twitched at the smell of fox. May reassured her, "it will go." She returned to filing a nail into shape, "you get use to it. They all love doing it. The other one they like is dead sheep." "Urgh." Lily pulled a face.

"It goes." George remarked as he came and sat down at the table and pulled his own face, "urgh, girlie stuff."

"Oh shut up. Everyone needs pampering occasionally." May retorted.

"What do I get?"

"The pleasure of our company." May teased and stuck her tongue out at her brother. He stuck his out back.

"No squabbling." Lily interrupted as she caught May pulling another face, "I think its my turn!" She stretched her mouth with her thumbs and stuck her tongue out. They all laughed again.

Lily found herself enjoying the evening more than she would have if she'd been out on the town. The best bit was it was free and she had ended up with her nails done as well. George brought out a green curry and sticky rice and dessert was a fruit salad and ice-cream. Over the food they found themselves regaling each other about their childhoods with May and George protesting at some of them. She also discovered they were twins with George being the elder by a couple of hours.

In the end George and the dogs left the girls talking and retreated to bed.
They giggled in front of the fire clutching hot chocolates overflowing with marshmallows while wrapped in Lily's soft blanket. With the man gone Lily remarked, "you seem close."

"Oh yes. We charged round the fields together. We had friends of course but its hard to see them outside of school in a farming community until we had transport otherwise there are a lot of fields to cross."

"Have you got a boyfriend?" Lily glanced sideways when May was quiet. "Not at the moment. George said you had one. What's he like?"

"Mac? He's a banker in London. He's handsome, a good laugh and good at sex." She drunkenly giggled, "he's coming up next week. You might get to meet him as he's staying the week. I'm quite excited. It's been two months and sometimes a phone call isn't enough." "What does he think of you doing this?"

"He's been really supportive." Lily lied too easily she realised as she went on, "he helped me get a good deal on a loan. And now I can live in the countryside and run a B&B and make and sell cheese and lamb. I can't believe my dream has come true. But what about yours? Have you always wanted to be a teacher?"

"Well," May blushed, "my dream is to travel the world but I will be happy just to see more of the UK. We've never really had a holiday as there has always been the farm to look after. Once I'm a teacher I can go anywhere."

"What is George's dream?"

"He's always been happy here. He loves the hills and mountains and as long as he's out on them he's happy. What he does want to do is become a sheepdog trial champion. Stan and Lou have been trained from the start for it."

"What's stopped him?"

May sobered up, "look at the time. We should go to bed." She finished her hot chocolate and then stood, "good night."

"Have I said something wrong?" Lily asked with concern.

"No, no. You haven't. Night."

May carefully walked up the stairs by nightlight to George's bedroom, forgetting she was meant to be sleeping on the sofa. She pulled off her shoes, jeans and jumper by the nightlight in his room- so that was how he kept he nightmares at bay. She saw the Bear Factory bear in its leather jacket that she had got for her twin brother and smiled as she slid into the spare side of the bed.

George woke in the morning to find May facing him, sleeping peacefully with a thumb in her mouth. He was a little surprised to see her but guessed she must have forgotten she was on the lumpy sofa. He slipped out of bed and untangled himself from the duvet as quietly as possible. He had a feeling both women were going to want bacon sandwiches for breakfast.

He found Lily asleep wrapped in her blanket in front of the dead stove and chuckled to himself as he passed through. He found a tray and sorted out plates and mugs for two.

He was making the sandwiches when the house phone rang. He looked round for it as he licked grease from his fingers. Finding it he answered, "Hillside Farm."

"Hello?"

"Hello?"

"Who's this? Where's Lily?" The voice on the other end demanded.

"I'll get her. Who is this?"

"Mac. Her boyfriend." The voice said pointedly.

"Hang on then." He placed the phone on the tray with the teas and bacon sandwiches.

Back in the sitting room he nudged Lily awake and waved a plate under her nose, "mmm, what's that smell? You are a star George." She sat up and eagerly took the plate and mug. "Mac is on the phone." He handed the phone over.

"What?! I'm not ready."

"Too late." He said as she took the phone and then left her.

Lily tentatively said, "hello?"

"Lily! Who the hell was that?" Mac demanded.

"Don't be paranoid. He's my farm manager." Lily reassured him.

"Can you afford him?"

"Aren't you going to ask how it's going instead?" She asked sourly. There was a sigh, "sorry, it's your money."

"And my dream." She pointed out, "I'm looking forward to see you next week. Are you still ok helping me put together the guest rooms?" "Of course I am. I said I would and then we can test out the beds." She giggled.

"Oh I miss you Lily."

"I miss you too."

"Are you sure you don't want to just come back to London?"

"I'm sure and I'm grateful for all your support."

"Mmm."

"Don't be like that. What have you been up to? You didn't answer your phone last night."

"I was out with the guys. But I got bored and came home. I think my phone ran out of power. You?"

"I had a really good one. George had his sister round and she stayed up with me and we had a girlie chat." She answered enthusiastically. "I'm glad you are starting to make friends."

"Mine are coming up once the rooms are ready."

"That'll be good."

"I've got to go. The ducks and chickens need feeding." She eyes were on the the cooling bacon sandwich. "Oh, ok."

"Love you."

"Love you too."

She hung up on Mac not really sure how to feel. He hadn't really understood her dream and it sounded like he still didn't. Hopefully she would convince him next weekend and then maybe he might be tempted to move away from the bright lights of London or maybe just closer. She downed the tea and ate her bacon sandwich.

4

Before Lily knew it Saturday had come round. She showered, did her legs and battled with her hair dryer. She was determined to look her best for Mac. She had even cleaned out the front of the Land Rover as she knew Mac would just pull a funny face if he had to sit in a dirty car. She carefully put her makeup on and then the only dress she had brought with her.

She put on her cleaned wellies as the day before George had dragged her into the fields. She had to learn about her little flock sooner or later. He had taken her up on the back of his quadbike, clinging to the bag of sheep feed tied to the back. He had borrowed the spare quadbike from the family farm. Stan and Lou had run alongside her.

She threw her bag across the Land Rover and then her heeled shoes. She planned to change into them when she got to the station where Mac would be in an hour. She hauled herself in and turned the engine on. It spluttered and protested but didn't start. She tried again, muttering to herself, "come on, come on."

When it wouldn't start she swore, "shit. This can't be happening." She jumped out, "George! George!" She wailed.

He ran out of a stable where he had been rummaging, "what?"

"It won't start. I'm meant to be going to Caenarfon to pick Mac up."

He crossed over to the Land Rover and lifted up the bonnet, "and very nice you look to. It looks like the battery."

She glared at him as it started to rain. She glared up at the sky and wailed, "this is not fair!"

"Calm down. I'll take you on the bike and then I'll come back and sort it out."

"How are we meant to get back?"

"Stay the night down in Caenarfon and take him out to a nice restaurant then
I'll pick you both up tomorrow."

Her eyes lit up, "great idea, but no dogs." She warned.

"No dogs?"

"He's not a fan of them." She admitted.

"Fair enough. You might want to put some trousers on and I'll go get ready and find my spare helmet."

"Thank you." She ran in to change.

It felt thrilling and exhilarating and scary all at the same time. She clung to George as he rode with the ease of a long-time rider. Her eyes were closed for most of the trip. With slightly shaky legs she got off when they came to a stop at the railway station next to the castle.

Mac, a tall man with an angular face topped with waxed ash blonde hair, was waiting with two bags for his week's stay. He saw his Lily get off the back of a motorbike- what was going on? Where was his ride? He eyed the guy on the bike through steely blue eyes. Who was he? He felt inferior when George pulled off his helmet and took Lily's from her. George barely looked at Mac. To Lily he said, "have a good time. Shall I meet you down here tomorrow?"   "I'll give you a ring."

"Not a problem." He pulled on his helmet, set the bike running and disappeared up the road leaving Mac staring in disbelief. Lily hugged him and gave him a kiss, "hiya lover boy."

"Who was that?"

"George. Come on."

"Where's your car?"

"The Land Rover's battery gave out. George suggested we stay in town overnight while he fixes it."

"I knew this was all a bad idea."

"Come on, it will be romantic." She pressed herself against him and slowly he softened. It was hard to resist her when she was being soppy.

"All right. It will be fun. Sooo, what is there to do in town?"

"A socking great big castle." She pointed behind him with a laugh.

He smiled, "I give in. Come on, lets go have some fun." He wrapped his arm round her shoulder, "lets see if we can find somewhere for my bags."

Up the road George was making his way to a local garage where he knew he would get a good price for a battery. He pulled up in front of the corrugated iron garage which looked like it might fall down. Daffodils were starting to peek out of planters and inside was as clean and tidy as a car mechanics could be. Outside the sign advertised what they could do under the name of Rhys' Cars.

He walked in with his gloves tucked into his helmet. The mechanic under a car high on a ramp turned at his footsteps. He lifted his safety goggles up and asked in Welsh, "George! Is that you?"

"Yes it is." George grinned, "how's life Davy?"

Davy abandoned emptying the oil from the car, "hey da, look who's come to visit. Oh man. I would hug you but I think I'm a bit oily." Though they were close he had felt a bit abandoned by his best friend recently so he was relieved to see him back especially as he had been at court the previous week and George hadn't wanted his support. He was relieved that the man was now behind bars even if it was only for a few years. Maybe the Menaces could be together again.

"That's all right. Actually, I'm here for a battery for Mr Lewis' old Land Rover."

"Hey George." The elder David popped his head out of the little office.

"Mr Rhys."

"How you doing? Where you working now?"

"Nearly there. I'm up at Hillside Farm. It's got a new owner."

"Excellent."

"Come out and have some drinks with us." Davy interjected as he went rummaging for a suitable battery.

"Can't do that. I've got to get this battery fitted and sort out the animals."

"Where's the owner?"

"In town with her boyfriend."

"All right, I'll come with you then. Is she a proper city girl? Why don't I see if the others want to come as well."

"Well… Oh go on."

"Brilliant. How's May?"

George rolled his eyes. Once Davy got an idea he was hard to stop, "May is good thanks."

"Are you going to let me ask her out now? I'll let you take Di out and we could do it as a double date."

"Take a breath Davy and no."

"Oh go on."

"No Davy."

"I'll go behind your back then." Davy teased as he pulled his blue gloves off, threw them in the bin and washed his hands before shrugging out of his overalls.

George sighed with a smile.

The elder David called out, "Davy, are you going to finish that car or are you abandoning it?"

"They don't need it till Tuesday da." Davy replied as he pulled his mobile out of his pocket, "let me do some ringing round and then we can go."   "Do you still have a helmet? I don't think you would fit May's though we could try." George teased.

"Cheeky. Oh hiya Moo. You fancy a get together at Georgie's new place."

"And Bugsy?" Moo asked on the end of the phone, "he's here with me. Oh, he wants to know if he can bring Susan with him."

"More the merrier." Davy grinned.

"Davy!" George exclaimed.

"Oh ssh. It's Bugsy's new girlfriend." Davy remarked with a wave of his hand,

"yeah, Hillside Farm, Lewis' old place. Bring some pizzas and beers."

"Why me?" Moo protested

"I'm going up with Georgie to sort out a battery."

"All right. You get the rounds in next time."

"See you later."

Between the two of them they got the battery changed just in time for a car to show up. Moo shouted out the window, "woo! Georgie! You can't keep away from us."

"We've got beer!" Bugsy shouted out of the other window.

"You so should have got May over as well." Davy cheekily remarked.

George threw an oily rag at him, "behave yourself or you'll have to do a Menace Dare."

Earlier he had been uncertain about having his friends round considering this wasn't really his home but Lily hadn't not said he couldn't have friends round. Anyway she was probably sprawled panting across some hotel bed with city boy Mac. He shook his head to get rid of the ugly image. He led the group inside.

They sat on the floor with the two dogs' noses inching closer to the rapidly cooling take away pizzas. None of the group cared as they were use to it. Looking round at them George was glad to have them as friends especially in the last few months when he and May had needed their good natured cheers and ribbing. Thinking about it they had got him through to the other side though recently he had stepped away from them as well. He hadn't been sure how they would all react if they got back together considering the high emotions that had been revealed so he was glad there didn't appear to be any differences.

Separated by Stan to his left was Davy, his best and oldest friend. It probably helped that their mothers were friends as well. Opposite him was blonde haired Bugsy who had gone to the same primary school and was also from a farming family. He'd ended up with the nickname from the thick lensed glasses he used to wear as his family hadn't been able to afford better, which had made him look bug eyed. Now he worked for the council and could afford better ones. Susan was apparently his new girlfriend but none of them currently knew much about her.

The last of the group was dark haired Moo, real name Morgan. He had joined the group at secondary school where he used to be bullied for smelling of cows so the rest of the Menaces had taken him under their wing. As for the group's name, well they had been a menace to the village with their escapades.

Moo pushed Lou away as she leant against him, eyes on the pizza slice, "get away Lou! That reminds me, are you actually going to remember to sign up for the trials this year?"

"You got me wasted last year. I was too hungover to remember." George pointed out.

"Yeah, that was a good night." Moo closed his eyes as he remembered.

"Oi, no snogging allowed." Davy pointed an accusing finger at Bugsy and

Susan. The pair blushed right up to their hairlines, plainly suited for each other. They continued holding hands but tried to pretend they hadn't been kissing.

"Hey Susan, any friends who might be interested in Georgie?" Moo asked, "he hasn't been laid for a while."

"Behave yourself Morgan Griffiths." Bugsy warned.

"Or what?" Moo dared.

"Why do you call him Georgie?" Susan dared ask.

"As in the rhyme, Georgie Porgie, pudding and pie, kissed the girls and made them cry." Davy answered. Susan's eyes widened.

"They didn't cry in a bad way." Bugsy reassured her, "basically they all wanted to go out with him. I think they mostly swooned. It's that Italian blood."

"Italian blood?" Susan asked in bewilderment.

"His great-grandfather was an Italian prisoner of war."

"Have you finished spoiling my street cred?" George asked as he drank from the bottle of beer and leant back against the sofa. He rubbed Stan's head behind the ears.

"What street cred?" Moo laughed, "you were and still are the unattainable hunk." George blushed.

"Even more so with your scars." Bugsy remarked and then realised he had said too much when the room went silent. The men glanced towards George to see how he would react. Davy came to the rescue by deciding, "I think that calls for a Menace Dare."

"Ah, come on guys. It was a slip of the tongue." Bugsy protested. He hadn't done one in a long time.

Davy glanced at George who was staring at his bottle intently and declared, "it has to be done in the name of Georgie's honour." Looking afraid, Susan asked, "what is a Menace Dare?"

"When one of us makes a tit out of themselves they get to be an even bigger tit. What shall it be Davy?" Moo answered.

"Is it raining?"

"Not at the moment but it will be cold."

"No sex for Susan tonight then." Davy announced and winked at Susan. She frowned at him but he just grinned back, "once round the yard bollocks naked."

"George!" Bugsy turned to him for mercy.

A small smile appeared on George's lips and Bugsy resigned himself to his fate. That evil little smile meant he wasn't going to escape his dare this time but if it brought his friend out of his blank stare he would do it. Acting the martyr Bugsy downed the last of his beer and began to undress. The dogs jumped up wondering what all the fun was about.

The group trooped out with Bugsy wrapped in Lily's blanket. Once in the yard Davy pulled the blanket off him, "off you go."

They all cheered as he began to run round the yard naked and trying to protect his bits. They all froze as the headlights of a car caught Bugsy. Gallantly he ran on. He wouldn't live it down if he stopped.

Inside the car Mac and Lily stared in disbelief as they saw the naked man run pass the headlights of the taxi. Mac exclaimed, "what the fuck?!" The taxi driver laughed, "oh ho. I'd love to know why Bugsy is doing that."

The car swung round to reveal the laughing group patting a shaking Bugsy on the back. The driver remarked to himself, "the Menaces are back together. It's good to see George enjoying himself again."

"Lily, you can't let this happen." Mac protested and at the driver, "what sort of name is Bugsy?"

Lily had heard the driver's comment. She leant forward, "what did you mean by that?"

The driver turned in his seat, "you don't know?"

"Don't know what?"

"It's not my place to say. He'll tell you when he's ready." Mac frowned, that didn't sound good. Was George a criminal? He would do some research when he got back to London with the help of a friend in the MET. He most certainly didn't want Lily living with a criminal. He was itching now to tell the group to grow up and snapped at the driver, "how much?" The driver was taken aback. He was about to halve the fare over the entertainment factor but not now. He decided to milk the city slick for the full fare, "fifty pounds."

"Fifty pounds?!"

"You're lucky I live in the village. You wouldn't have got anyone else coming out this far on a one way trip this far out."

"Just pay him." Lily said softly. She was too tired for arguments.

As Mac paid with a hmpfh and got his bags Lily got out. She found
George alone and asked, "where are your friends?"

"Sorry. You never said I couldn't." George blushed, "and I thought you were staying in town tonight."

"That's alright, those rooms are your home. Mac didn't like any of the options so we had dinner then found a taxi. Are they staying?"

"We'll be quiet."

"You should consider this a warning. This is not your property to do with as you wish. You should ask permission first." Mac declared as he joined Lily and George
George opened his mouth and then close it again as he recognised a bully in the banker.

"Ssh Mac. I'll handle it." Lily put a hand on Mac's arm. She recognised the signs in him that he was tired and to be fair he had been travelling most of the day.

"They'll be gone in the morning." George remarked stiffly. "Good." Mac sniffed and then disappeared inside.

"It looked like you were having a good time." Lily commented with a smile, "you'll have to tell me later what on earth was going on." He smiled his little smile and her heart skipped a beat, "cause."

"Good night."

"Night." He stepped out of her way. He watched her walk in and wondered how she had ended up with a man whose first impressions were that of an overbearing killjoy. Maybe in the morning he would be better.

He returned to his end where they were all giggling. He narrowed his eyes as Davy blurted out, "ooh, Georgie's in trouble."

"No I'm not."

"He didn't seem very nice." Moo remarked as he rubbed Lou's belly.

"She was pretty." Davy teased and gave George a nudge.

"Be careful or you might have to do a dare." George replied in jest, "she's got a boyfriend and is also my employer. I hope you haven't been conspiring with May?"

"Did she have the same idea?" Davy's ears, if he had collie ones, would have pricked up, "see, we are destined to be together."

"Keep trying." George laughed.

Davy pulled a face, "it was worth a try."

"Come on, it's late. I think it's time to go to bed. Bugsy, you and Susan can have my room if you want but no funny business."

Bugsy brightened, "cheers mate. Come on Susan."

Once upstairs as she snuggled into her boyfriend after he had turned off the night light she asked, "where did he get the scars on his wrist?"

"I can't really tell you." He replied after a moment battling with his conscious, "lets just say if we had known where he was going we would have been there with him and maybe he wouldn't have been so badly injured." "Oh. You are all so loyal to each other." She remarked sleepily. "We've known each other too long not to be." He commented softly and kissed the top of her head.

Downstairs with quiet jibes the others moved the furniture around and pumped up Moo's large airbed, a must for any of their sleepovers as long as it didn't deflate and that had happened a few times. With pillows, blankets and a sleeping bag the three men piled on and had to push the dogs off. When they were young there would have been space to make it a human and canine heap but not any more.

5

Mac leant against the door frame of the empty stable which had been turned into a shed long ago and Lily had unwittingly brought all the junk in it. It was all stuff that might prove useful in the future for making pens, and fixing gates and walls. He took a puff of his cigarillo and brushed a hand through his ash blonde hair. He watched George mending a gate. The Welshman glanced over and muttered to himself.

Finishing his cigarillo Mac flicked it away and entered the shed. He held out a hand, "I think we got off on the wrong foot the other night. The names Macintosh McGuire, Mac for short."

George rubbed his hand down his overalls before taking Mac's hand, "George Risoll."

"It's quite big in here isn't it?" Mac remarked as he put his hands in his jean's pockets and carefully walked round the piles of wood, chicken wire and barbed wire. He turned back to George, "I think Lily's barking up the wrong tree. A space like this and if the other building is like this as well she should turn them into holiday cottages. Is there much need for them around here? Do they make much money?"

George looked up, "she wants this as a farm."

"Come on," Mac picked up George's hammer, studied it and put it back down again, "I know and you definitely do know there's no money in farming. Look at the crap around you. Everything gets kept for just in case. I've seen it, everything gets held together with string. Look at you, fixing this gate to save money. I could buy plenty of new ones if I wanted."

George reached for the hammer and gritted his teeth. This man didn't have a clue about why people chose to farm. Carefully he said, "we are the backbone of this country. We put food and milk in the shops. There would soon be none without us."

"Actually it's the banks keeping the country afloat." George wordlessly walked out with the dogs following.

In the house Lily was at the table chewing on a pen. She was trying to do some paperwork but her mind was distracted. She found herself thinking about George in a hot country with only a pair of swimming shorts on and sweeping her off her feet and…

There was welsh swearing, "prick."

And that was the end of that. She heard him stomping around the kitchen and shouted, "boots!"

She heard the voice recede with more welsh muttered swearing. Two filthy dogs ran in and she shouted, "dogs!"

"Stan! Lou!"

The two collies turned and bound into hall where she heard the three of them leave. She wondered what had got him annoyed but she was also relieved he hadn't come in. He would probably have caught her blushing at the thoughts she had been happening. What was worse was she was doing it while Mac was staying. She muttered to herself, "I love Mac, I love Mac."

She frowned, where was Mac? She remembered sending him outside to smoke. He was meant to be helping her put furniture together so she could make her website live with photos.

All George had wanted was a mug of tea which he would have taken with him while he hid in the stables. 'Mac for short' was a pompous prick and really didn't understand life in the country. He probably saw the food on the shelves or on his plate and didn't really care about all the man hours and love that it took to get it on the shelf or plate. He grumbled away to himself as he started to brush the two ponies. The dogs wandered out. He was glad that Mac hadn't seen him working with dogs as he would probably have scoffed at that as well. He would be glad to see the back of him at the end of the week,

As brushing the ponies began to soothe him he began to feel foolish. Why was he letting Mac get to him. No one was going to ever change his love of the hills and valleys of North Wales. The only time his heart felt torn was when May talked about leaving. He wondered whether their connections as twins would survive. It had certainly got them through the last few months.

6

It was with relief that George watched Mac being taken to the station by Lily. He was sick of tinned soup. He headed up the hill to check the sheep as one hadn't looked very well. The dogs clung to the back of the quad bike. He found the ewe on its side, clearly dead. With hands on hips he said to the dogs sniffing around, "there's always one. Get awff you varmits." He pushed Stan out of the way with a foot.

In the Land Rover Lily gritted her teeth as she crunched the gears. Mac was on his phone, "hey, you've had a visitor already."

"Have I?" She tried to peer over his arm before swerving back into lane. They fell back into silence.

At the station Mac held her close and gave her a long kiss. As he broke away he smiled his soppiest smile and gave her bum a cheeky squeeze, "to remember me by."

"Cheeky." She smiled back but it disappeared when his back was turned. She called out, "ring me when you get back." He waved a hand.

She sat down behind the steering wheel with a sigh. Was it wrong of her to be relieved that he was off back to London? Until now she had not realised how demanding he could be. Over the week there had been a slight sneer whenever she talked about her plans with him. However, she was more determined than ever to prove to Mac she could make her dreams work out. Hopefully her friends would be more supportive when they came and helped her by pretending to be guests. Two weeks to go. That brightened her mood for a few minutes. And now that the rooms were ready it was time to actually start learning more about the animals in her care.

But first she felt George needed a thanks for putting up with Mac being difficult. She wandered the town looking for inspiration but gave up. She didn't know how he would react to either a serious gift or even a jokey one. She knew what he probably would like but currently she couldn't afford to do it- a kitchen of his own.

Getting home Lily found George sitting in the garden, a mug of tea in one hand, with his eyes closed. It was still chilly but at least the sun was out so he had decided to enjoy it. She dropped on to the seat beside him, "ooh, this is nice. Chocolate?"

She offered him the chocolate bar; her poor gift, the best she could come up with.

He frowned, "err, thanks." He opened his eyes briefly and then closed them again," did he get on the train alright?"

She gave Lou a stroke as the dog placed her head on her knee, "yeah. I'm sorry if he was a bit… well..." She tried to come up with the right word.

"Prick." George answered in Welsh.

"What?" Some day she'll start to understand a few words.

"I know what you mean." He added in english, "it's alright. You'll just need to prove him wrong."

"That is true. Don't be afraid to let your friends visit. I think it was more the shock of seeing one running around naked." George chuckled, "yes, one of our dares."

"Dares?"

"If one of us makes a tit of ourselves then they have to make up for it by being an even bigger one."

"I get you. What did he say?"

George paused before replying, "just something a bit close to the heart." Brightening, "perhaps it's time you had a dare of your own but not because you have made a tit of yourself."

"And that is why I am sitting here." She watched him gulp down some of his tea. Oh; if only she could nuzzle into his neck. She shook her head to get rid of the alluring vision. Was it just her or did others get the same thoughts? She would have to see how her London friends would react at the sight of him. "It's a bit late today but could you take me out tomorrow and show me what you do."

"Course. Just to warn you we are heading towards the most tiring but exciting time of year." He smiled.

"Lambs?"

"Yeap."

"From this side that sounds scary."

"Most go without a hitch and all you get to see is the wagging tails as they feed from mum."

"How long have you been doing it?"

"Since I was about ten. Mainly observing for the first few years except when my small hands came in useful."

"A pro then?" She teased.

"Always time to learn more. These are sheep, they do like to spring surprises on you. You've lost one today."

"How come?"

"God knows but sometimes they like to just keel over." He replied matter of factly, "now did you do some shopping. I don't think I could live another day on tinned soup."

"It will be nice to eat in and not have beans on toast al a George."   "You served him that?" He asked with surprise.   "Yes." She said with pride, "though it was al a Rarebit."   "And how did he take it?" He was curious now.

"He was impressed."

"We'll make a cook out of you yet." He grinned.

"Maybe cooked breakfasts first." She remarked with a grin back, "we have already had our first visitor to the website."

"Well done, you'll have to show me the website later."

7

Two weeks flew by. By the end of them she had just about mastered the quad bike without slamming on the brakes and going over the handlebars. The dogs eyed her warily if she got into the driving seat before resigning themselves to walking with their master. She had also watched George split off the pregnant ewes into a field closer to the farm with sheepdog herding skills that clearly came naturally to him. She frowned as she watched the dogs, "is Lou alright?
She seems to be moving slower."

"Oh, should have said. I think I'll be having puppies as well as your lambs to contend with." He grinned.

"Congratulations." She gave him an awkward sideways hug.

"I'll make some good money out of the pups."

"Has she had puppies before?"

"This is her second litter." He informed her, "they come from good stock and all the locals know what a good pair they are." He went on with pride.

"You said you do sheepdog trials?"

"Yeah. Missed a few last year which pulled my ranking down. I'm not going to let it happen this time." He said with determination as he looked out across the valley, "right, enough chatting; lets go see how your ewes are doing."

She began to learn what to look for in a pregnant ewe and had a go at feeling their abdomens close to their udders but it all felt the same to her. However she could see, when pointed out by George, that they all looked a bit lopsided which was a good sign though not a guarantee that the ewes were carrying. She asked, "how long?"

"Couple more weeks yet according to Mr Lewis' dates but who knows. If we do get an early one then we will have to bring it in so we don't lose the lamb."

"Ok." She sat on the large wooden five bar gate with George leaning against it. They stayed like it for a while admiring the view. She still couldn't believe her luck in getting such a scenic place even if it rained more often then not.

Thankfully there had been barely any snow.

She buried her face in her scarf as the wind picked up. She couldn't resist the urge to swing her welly-booted feet like a little girl who's seat was too high.

She giggled to herself.

She started to feel herself slip off the slick gate and just about managed to rescue herself. She still ended up with mud all the way up her back from landing in a large muddy puddle. George laughed.

"It's not that funny." She pouted.

"It is when you've tried to stay clean the whole time."

"Take this then." She kicked the muddy water at George who got the spray from it. He tried to protect himself and failed.

"What was that for?" He protested.

She just grinned and ran off down the hill but the grass was slick and muddy and she landed on her backside again.

Seeing her fall George ran down the field. Reaching her he asked with concern, "are you alright?"

"Help me up will you." She reached up an arm but instead of him pulling her up he slipped himself and landed in the mud beside her. She smeared mud across her face as she brushed her hair out of her eyes. She laughed. She couldn't explain why but it all felt ridiculous hilarious, sitting in the mud next to a man she was still pretending she didn't fancy.

"What's funny?"

"Oh, oh." She gasped and clutched at her side. She had laughed so hard she had given herself a stitch, "nothing. I don't really know why I am laughing." "Well, you've got mud on your face." He pulled out a rag from a pocket and tried to clean the mud off her forehead but it didn't work.

They both froze when they realised what had just happened. His touch had sent a shiver down her spine. Breaking the tension she whispered, "I have a boyfriend and I love him."

"I know." He whispered back as he shoved the rag back in his pocket.

"Oh, look, I think its nearly time to feed the ducks and chickens." She said a bit too loudly as she got to her feet and almost fell down again. She tried not to look at George's face.

"Yes definitely. Time to get dinner sorted." He hastily agreed in the same loud voice as hers though there was no one to see or hear them.

Reaching the house they turned their backs on each other as they pulled off muddy clothes. Lily couldn't resist having a peak. She bent down to gather up her clothes to put in the washing machine. She glanced round then and saw his t-shirt ride up revealing a tanned body with a large scar on his side. The scar still looked quite new. She bit her lip, did she dare ask?

She looked away as he reached for his overalls and handed them to her. She felt sure she was blushing as if he had caught her looking. She stood there, clutching the clothes to her body for modesty's sake as he headed through to his rooms.

Over dinner he asked, "when do your friends come?"

"Friday. They're coming up by train."

"Do you want me to pick them up?"

"Why?"

"Remember you said I could borrow the Land Rover. I've got to take Lou to the vets."

"Oh right. That would be great actually."

Friday came and George appeared in the kitchen dressed to go out. She had got so use to seeing him in his overalls and then in the evening whatever he had to hand that she was surprised by how smart he could look. He remarked, "I thought I'd best look half decent for picking up your friends."

"I think you'll definitely impress them." She grinned as she took in the trousers, boots and shirt. She teased, "where's the hat cowboy?" He rolled his eyes, "a woolly hat will do."

"Spoilsport."

"Anyway… Hang on, what are you up to?" He stared round the kitchen. It appeared a bag of flour, make that several bags, had exploded. The counter was covered in it and so was Lily. She blushed, "attempting to make a cake."

"Is there actually any flour in it?"

"Yes." She scowled. Changing the subject she asked, "what did you want?"

"Don't expect me to clear it up. Anyway, what I was going to say was can you look after Stan? He's not brilliant on his own. Just keep him shut in a room for ten minutes otherwise he'll try following. He's clean, well, the mud is dry."

"Okay."

"Cheers." He grabbed the keys from the hook and herded Stan into the dining room and shut him in. Stan began whining and then let out a howl as Lou walked out with George. Lily glanced at the door as Stan scrabbled at the door. George reassured her, "he'll stop in a bit. I'll give you a ring when I've picked them up. It'll give you plenty of time to clear this place up." He hinted. He waved a hand as he walked out of the house.

Stan barked at the front door just before she then heard a car drive into the yard. She frowned as she glanced at the clock. She wasn't expecting him back yet, he hadn't rung. She went to the door and stood on the porch step as Stan pushed past.

Sarah was hanging out of the passenger window waving a bottle of champagne, "Lillyy! Surprise!"
Lily glanced down, she so wasn't ready for them. She was wearing her scruffiest clothes. She pulled on her boots and came out to greet them.

All the girls climbed out of the car and crowded around Lily. Lily couldn't believe they were all here, "what a surprise. I thought you were coming by train?"

"We wanted to surprise you." Sarah declared.

"It's a good thing that I hadn't gone to the station then." She pointed out but then grinned, "oh I'm so glad you've all come." And they all hugged each other. Stan jumped around them barking. She gestured to the door, "come on in. Down Stan. I just need to let George know you are here."   "Who's George?" Becca asked.

"My farm manager, farmhand and shepherd."

"God, he must be old."

"He isn't."

"Who wants champagne? Got any glasses Lily?" Sarah shouted from the kitchen. Her head popped round the door, "why is there flour everywhere?
What's that burning smell?"

"Oh shoot!" Lily flew through the kitchen to the aga.

"Were you trying to bake?" Becca exclaimed.

"Yes."

"Can you cook yet?" Claire followed Lily into the dining room and watched Lily pull the cake from the aga.

"No." Lily replied.

"Are you still living on beans?"

"Don't be silly. You know I'm not."

The three women couldn't help staring when George entered. They glanced at each other and then at Lily. They had so expected an older man not what they would definitely class as a hunk and apparently he could cook as well. He blushed at the attention, "I'm just here to claim Stan."

"How was the vets?" Lily asked from the table.

"Lou's coming along just fine. We could see about four puppies but you never really know."

"Girls. This is George."

He waved as they all sang, "hi George."

"Don't run away on our account." Claire fluttered her eyes at him. She was disappointed when he barely noticed and remarked to them, "it's all right. You have fun catching up. See you in the morning."

The women looked to Lily once he had gone. Claire couldn't believe her seduction trick had failed. Becca exclaimed, "you've kept quiet about him. Why didn't you tell us? What has Mac said about him?" "Mac is fine and I have told you about him."

"Not how good looking he is." Becca protested. Claire leant across the table and as she reached for an olive she asked, "is he gay?"

"Umm." Lily remembered May mentioning that he had had a few girlfriends, "no, he's not."

"Does he have a girlfriend?" Claire eagerly asked.

"Umm, not that I'm aware of."

"Awesome." They might only be up for the weekend but that wasn't going to stop her flirting with him. As far as she was aware farmers were always up for a tumble in the hay.

Lily looked uncertainly at Claire. She didn't like the idea of Claire getting her claws into George. She didn't know why considering she had Mac. "We are meant to be here for our friend, not for you to have a shag with a country bumpkin." Sarah pointed out to Claire.

"Spoilsport." Claire replied, "just because you can never get any action."

"Not fair. I'm too busy, that's all."

"Calm down. Don't fight." Becca interrupted, "what's for pud Lily?"

"Well it was going to be cake but it will just have to be ice-cream."

"Have you got any sauces?"

"Probably."

"Lets make sundaes then and eat them in front of the fire."

"Sounds like a plan." Sarah remarked cheerfully. The other two chorused their agreements. Becca had once again soothed the dented egos and Lily smiled a thanks at her.

Claire smoothed her bleach blonde hair, checked her make-up in the mirror and blew herself a kiss. She modelled herself on Marilyn Monroe. No man had ever failed to fall for her charms, and she wasn't going to let George be the first. She checked her outfit again, as tight as possible without looking like a whore. She slipped out of the house and headed towards the shed she had seen George enter.

She leant against the door, "hello handsome." He glanced over and found himself doing a double take, "umm, morning." She entered the shed, "what you doing?" She approached him and came in close. He took a sidestep and eyed her warily. She asked, "would you like some help?"

"I'm just feeding the birds. Here, you feed them." He handed her a bucket, "and I'll collect the eggs for breakfast."

"Ooh, breakfast." She smiled, "how hard do you like your eggs?" He frowned and shook his head. Had she really tried to come on to him by referencing eggs? He gestured her out, "lead the way."

She wiggled her bum as she walked out. No man could resist her wiggle. She glanced behind and caught him watching. He blushed. She fluttered her eyelashes. One more move and she would have him. She didn't have the time to be subtle.

She scattered the chicken feed as George went looking for eggs. She kept her eye out for when he came out. Seeing him come out she crossed and purposely slipped, falling towards him. He grabbed her, "you alright?" She looked up into his face, "oh thank you. I wouldn't want to ruin my nice clothes."

"Umm, no." He felt uncomfortable. He looked around for an escape route. He had been hit on a few times but this was too full on. He let go of her, "come on; Lily needs to test her breakfast out on all of you." Claire glowered at his back. Maybe he was actually gay. She had failed.

Lily's friends decided to be as awkward as possible. They all requested different eggs. She couldn't believe her friends and especially Claire. She had seen her walk in with George but was also relieved he didn't seem to have become absorbed by her. He tried to stay out of the way but soon saw her floundering at the cooker. He could hear her swearing to herself. Finishing his toast he stepped in, "what can I do to help?"

"Eggs." She stepped out of the way.

"Everything all right in there?" Becca called out.

"Yes." Lily said with a forced smile.

The women laughed. It may appear cruel but they knew it would only benefit Lily in the long run.

A cheer rose up when Lily and George came out with their plates and toast. The hosts retreated to the kitchen. Lily sagged against the counter, relieved it was over for the moment. George patted her on the shoulder, "you haven't done too badly. Where's mine?" He teasingly ended.

She threw her tea-towel at him, "make your own."

They both turned when they heard a knock at the door. George said, "I'll get it."

The phone rang and Lily exclaimed with a laugh, "I'll get that."

"More coffee." Her friends chorused.

"Ssh." Lily hissed as she grabbed the phone. Answering she said, "good morning, Hillside Farm." The women craned to hear.

"Yes it is romantic. There are the hills and Snowdonia for walking and Caernarfon is nearby as well… I'm sure we could do dinner for you for a little extra… Yes that is fine. I'll see you then, then. Bye." She turned to her friends as she hung up and grinned, "my first booking."

"Yeah!" They cried out and then Sarah asked, "can we get some more coffee now?"

"Now you can but let me write this down before I forget." George shouted, "Lily, what have you been ordering?"

She peered out into the hallway, "umm. Cheese making stuff."

"Cheese making?" He frowned as he put the two parcels on the floor.

"Remember. No, well… when the ewes have got some milk could you get me some of their milk?"

"Can't you get the hang of one thing at a time?" George protested, "we're not set up for milking. I've never hand milked a cow, let alone a sheep." Lily pretended to sulk.

"I'm going out." George remarked, exasperated by Lily. He pulled his boots back on and left.

Lily was left staring at the back door a little shocked by his reaction. That was the first time she had really seen him grumpy.

George left the women to their own devices by meeting with Moo and Davy at their local pub. They sat in the corner nursing their pints over a few bags of nuts which that and crisps was all the pub sold. As he reached for some more nuts George remarked, "she's a crazy woman. She now wants me to milk the sheep. Does your mum know how to milk by hand Moo? Any chance she can teach me?"

"I think Grandda does. I'll ask."

"Thanks."

The pub suddenly went quiet and they turned in their seats to see what was going on. Lily and her friends had just walked through the door. Though they weren't dressed up it was still obvious that they weren't from the area. Lily shifted uncomfortably as they approached the bar. This was so clearly a locals' pub. Several of the men and women had dogs at their feet. They stared warily at these bright city girls chatting away.

Claire looked round. This was all so quaint to her. She spotted George hidden in the corner with his friends, "ooh look; George is here."

"Oh no." George muttered in Welsh and shrank down in his seat, "she's the one I was telling you about."

Davy grinned, "she's hot."

"You're welcome to her."

Claire minced over and sat down next to George on the bench, determined to get George to notice her, "shift up." She pressed herself against him and reluctantly he moved across only to give himself some space.

"I see what you mean." Davy laughed in Welsh.

"What?" Claire looked over and fluttered her eyelashes.

"Nothing. Hi Lily, sorry about last time." Davy answered as Lily sat down beside him.

"Sorry to intrude. They wanted to come out and they heard that George was coming here so wanted to come see."

"So George, are you going to introduce us to your friends?" Claire slid a hand over his thigh. He stiffened. He moved his thigh and cleared his throat with a cough, "umm, well, this is Moo… Morgan and Davy."

"Hello." She smiled sweetly at the other two while her friends rolled their eyes. Here she went again but at least for once her seduction attempts weren't working very well so it was turning out to be quite amusing. By now she would normally be snogging her victim of the night. Lily could see how uncomfortable George was with her friend's very forward approach.

It turned into a good night in the end especially when Moo pulled out a pack of cards. They ended up staying to last call. Though she hadn't really wanted to come to the pub she was glad that her friends had demanded she drove them there. A few more of the younger generation joined them, attracted by the fresh conversation happening. Claire remained single minded in trying to get into George's trousers even though he was trying to ignore her to start with and then politely told her he wasn't interest.

When the pub closed she had one last attempt, "can I come home with you Georgie?"

"It's George." He reminded her again. Only his friends were allowed to call him that.

"Whatever. I've never been on a motorbike." She wrapped her hands round his arm.

"Claire, leave him alone." Sarah called out, "come on Lily wants to go."   "I only have my helmet and I think you've had too much to drink so I'd rather you didn't." He rescued his arm as Sarah came to rescue him from Claire. Behind the scene Moo and Davy were in silent stitches.

They had half turned round to hide it but with the girls gone they approached George. They laughed out loud.

"It's not funny." George protested.

"It so is." They laughed as they leant against each other to stay standing. Moo wiped a tear from his eye, "I've never had so much fun. Oh she so wanted you to get in her knickers. Any longer and I think she would have stripped off, ripped your clothes off and fucked you anyway."

"You have such a way with women." Davy added. George glared at his friends and then couldn't help laughing as well at the hilariousness of the situation.

"When do they go?" Davy asked.

"Monday."

"Let us know if she finally gets what she wants."

"I'm just going to hide with the sheep."

"Come on Davy, I'll drop you off." Moo said having now sobered up, "take care of yourself George."

"Will do." He waved them off.

He pulled into a passing place on his way home. He would give Claire a chance to go to bed so she didn't try getting into his. It was an impressively clear night and he looked across the dark fields at the stars and moon. Maybe it was time to find a new girlfriend. It had been a long while now since he had had one. He definitely was not thinking of Claire. A smiling Lily from breakfast flashed into his mind. His mind was right, Lily was more than enough at the moment. It was almost like they were together already considering the amount of time they spent together. With his head clear and a decision made he put the bike back into gear and headed home to the dogs and bed.

8

There may have only been about fourteen pregnant ewes to keep an eye on but it was still knackering having to check on them every four hours. Lily came with him for a few checks. He tried to show her what she should be looking out for but she kept getting distracted by the new born lambs especially if they were on their feet feeding and wagging their tails.

To add to the stress Lou had found herself a half-hidden spot behind the sofa to create her den. He helped her by adding some old blankets for her to nestle into. And just like the ewes he was checking on her every four hours. As well as that he needed to come up with a birthday present for May. He wanted to do something special for her this year to show that the last year and a half was truly over. Once the lambing was over they would be able to celebrate their birthday which always coincided with lambing every year.

He was struggling to come up with anything. He'd already sent the now traditional bouquet of flowers to her and he had received in return another square to the quilt she was making for him. They been doing the same thing for the last ten years with her planning to give him the quilt once he got married. The thing was she forgot every year what she had done the last so every square so far had a sheep on it.

He was puzzling over what to do as he was knelt in the straw with his arm up the backside of a straining ewe. The head had been coming out before the legs. He had pushed the head back in and hooked his fingers round the front legs to bring them out. He sat back, cleaning his bloody arm on some straw. He watched as the wild-eyed ewe strained and pushed and before long the lamb came out.

Maybe he should just take her out for a ride with a picnic. He liked the feel of that idea and smiled to himself. He looked up as he heard footsteps.

May leant over the pen and in Welsh said, "I thought I would find you here. Happy Birthday."

"Happy Birthday to you too." He replied in Welsh.

"Thanks for the flowers as usual."

"Glad you liked them."

"Mum and lamb all right?" She gestured at his blood smeared arm.

"Yeah. The lamb is fine. What are you doing here anyway?"

"Just wanted to see my brother."

They both looked to the door as they heard footsteps. Lily stepped in,

"George? Oh, hi May. Oh there you are."

"What is it?" George asked as he stood up.

"I think Lou is in labour." Lily answered.

"All right I'm coming.

"I'm coming too." May declared eager to see how Lou and Stan's puppies would come out.

Stan was locked out of the sitting room much to his outrage. He whined at the door. May made tea for everyone as George adjusted the sofa to observe and Lily hung back. Lou wagged her tail limply. George stroked her head, "it's all right girl."

By the evening five puppies had been born, licked clean and were now suckling. Stan was allowed back in and under supervision sniffed at Lou and the puppies. The girls leant over the sofa looking down while cooing. Lily asked, "what are you going to do with them?"

"Keep them."

Lily looked horrified. The thought of seven muddy dogs was too much. May and George laughed at the expression on her face.

"Don't be silly. He'll sell them. They come from good parents and well known grandparents so he'll get some decent money for them." May consoled her. She bounced on the sofa, "come on Georgie, are you free now?"

"For the moment. Let me check the barn and then I'm all yours."

Lily looked between brother and sister, "what's going on?"

"Nothing scary. Just here to take my brother out for a drink." May smiled and then to her brother she remarked, "any longer and it will be pointless going out. Come on, it's our birthday."

"Your birthdays?"

"We'll celebrate properly with friends and family once lambing is over. Come on Georgie."

"Why don't you stay instead and I'll break open a bottle of wine." May looked at her brother with a raised eyebrow. He shrugged his shoulders and said in Welsh, "up to you?"

"Well, why not. Last time was not good fun." May replied and turned to Lily, "let's do it."

Before any of them realised it a party was being planned for a few weeks' time. May loved the idea. They hadn't had a good party for a while.

Before she knew it Lily found herself hosting the party but with May's contacts it didn't get too expensive. Someone brought the hog roast. George's friends put up a marquee as showers had been forecast. The twins' mother sorted out a cake- chocolate for May and in the shape of a sheep for George. It was the same cake they'd had every year since they were five. For drinks everyone was told to bring their own along with seating.

From the marquee Lily looked on as young and old enjoyed themselves. It looked like the whole community had abandoned their farms and animals to come and eat, drink, talk and dance. Those of her age sat around wrapped in coats and blankets talking while the elders had moved indoors to the warmth of the Aga. The children had disappeared to the sitting room to fall asleep in front of late evening telly. Everyone was stuffed with pig but it didn't stop them from drifting across to what was left to pick at it.

George and May's mother, Hester, appeared at Lily's side with two cups of tea. Handing one over she smiled softly, "I think you are now definitely part of the community. Thank you for doing this."

"To be honest it was mainly May." Lily replied as she realised George had his mother's smile.

"I think we have needed this. We've all needed to put the last year behind us. I haven't seen May so happy in a while."

That took Lily by surprise since the few times she had seen May she seemed happy in herself, "what do you mean? What happened?"

The older lady shook her head and walked off leaving Lily bemused. They kept implying something but then wouldn't talk about it. Clearly something traumatic had happened to the twins but what? She was pulled out of her thoughts by Moo shouting, "hey Lily, come and join us."

"Coming."

She squeezed on a garden bench between George and Moo. The group grinned at her. She eyed them suspiciously. What were they about to do? Moo raised his bottle of beer, "I believe we should give our gracious hostess a toast in thanks for putting up with all of us."

"Here, here." Everyone raised their bottles and glasses.

"And here's to a fresh start for Georgie and May."

"Here, here."

May and George glanced knowingly at each other. They raised their glass and bottle at each other. No one paid attention as they all went back to their conversations.

Davy took his moment when George left the group. He walked round to where May sat with her friends. He hadn't been able to take his eyes off her all evening. With some dutch courage in him he coughed to get her attention. She turned to him and looked up, light from the house reflecting in her eyes, "are you alright Davy?"

"Umm, yeah. Umm, would you like to take a little walk?" He showed her his torch. He thought he saw her whole face light up when she smiled, "not at all."
She got up as the group wolf whistled and began singing, "May and Davy
sitting in a tree..."

"Infantile." Davy protested as he blushed. They all knew he had fancied May for a few years but hadn't made a move out of respect for his best friend. She wrapped her arms round one of his, comfortable within his company.

"Ignore them." She smiled shyly, "where do you want to go?"

"Down to the barn. We can say we were checking on the ill ewe."

"Lead the way then."

They walked in silence till they entered the yard where Davy asked, "how has life been?"

"Good actually. Did you really get Bugsy to run round this yard naked?"

"Yeah." Davy grinned, "I think we surprised Mr Green."

"I wish I had been there."

"It's good to see you smiling again."
She looked up into his face and saw his adoration for her. She smiled, "its good to be able to again. And it's good to be learning to be a teacher again. The therapist says I'm doing well though it's still hard to talk about it all. I should have listened to all of you especially Georgie." She leant in

against Davy. He got his arm back and cautiously put it around her shoulders as she continued, "I think Georgie is okay as well. What do you think?"

"He's keeping himself busy. He was in a bad way May. He doesn't talk about it. I don't know if that is a good or bad thing." He stopped walking and turned to look at May. He cleared his throat, "May, I… umm, would you like to go out with me?"

"Like on a date?"

He nodded, "if you don't feel ready to I will understand."

"No. I would like to give it a try." She leant up to kiss him on the cheek. He turned his head and she found herself kissing his lips. She broke away in surprise and he grinned. She laughed- cheeky sod. But it had felt good. Did she dare do it again? She looked up and his eyes looked at her with concern. She wondered why she hadn't realised how much he cared before. Then she realised why- he was George's best friend. Did she dare open her heart again? She looked into Davy's warm face again and realised he would never harm her. She took hold of his face and kissed him. He wrapped his arms round her and held her tight. As she broke off he softly said, "I will never harm you."

"I know. Can we not tell Georgie yet?"

"I was going to say the same thing."

She giggled, "come on, we should go back before he starts to suspect anything." She took his hand for the walk across the yard.

"Shall I ring you later in the week?"

"Yes."

Back in the garden George didn't notice that his best friend and sister were missing. He was talking to his mother and older brother, "it's all good here. I've got interest in two of the puppies already."

"I saw them earlier, they are adorable." Hester remarked.

"She's not working you too hard is she?" Albert asked.

"No." George replied.

"You're not working yourself too hard." Their mother said with concern. "The hardest bit is going to be the shearing." George admitted.

"Albert will help you."

"Cause I will. Give me a shout closer to the time to remind me." Albert confirmed.

The Risolls were the last to go. George and May exchanged their gifts at the last moment. They laughed when he opened his to reveal a new outfit for his bear. May explained, "like earlier, now is a new start."

"You being back with us is more than enough." He replied with a hug, "open mine when you get home."

"I will Georgie."

As he watched them drive off Lily appeared and remarked, "never thought I'd be holding such a big party."

"Everyone really enjoyed it."

"George?"

"Mmm." He took the offered mug of tea.

She hesitated. Was now really the time to ask about other people's cryptic comments? It hadn't just been the twins' mother, others had also made vague references to some event that had happened before she arrived. She changed her mind at the last second, "your turn to do the washing up." "What happened to the dishwasher?" He turned to her in horror.

"Nothing. Come on, time for bed. We have a farm to run. What happens now that lambing is done?" She walked off.

"Shearing when the weather warms up. I'm going to see to the dogs and then head to bed. Sheepdog trials are starting as well so I might need to borrow the Land Rover."

"Fine by me. Night." She waved a tired hand.

He watched her go. She was a strange one sometimes. He chuckled to himself as he locked the front door.

9

It was breakfast time for the guests who were occupying all three bedrooms. Lily had now got the hand of cooking breakfasts as she moved round the kitchen with confidence as George watched the toast. Outside Stan and Lou were being bothered by their last puppy. As she plated up Lily glanced over at George, "hey, you are meant to be serving the toast, not eating it. They need big breakfasts as they are off to Snowdon."

"I was wondering why they were up at the same time as me. You know, if you didn't want me to eat their toast you could give me a kitchen." He helped her carry the plates into the Morning Room in his socked feet and biker leathers.

"But you would miss me." She bantered straight back, "I thought you were selling all the puppies? Why do you still have one?"

"Well, I can explain that." He smiled cheekily, "if you are going to be a sheep farmer you need a dog."
She turned, stunned, "is she mine?"

"Yes. Happy with that?"

"Oh yes. Will you help me train her?"

"Of course. She's here as a working dog. You've proven yourself capable of herding them though you only have the twenty-seven sheep."

"I'll have to come up with a name."

"You will. I'm going to make a move." He finished his tea.

"Enjoy your day. Anything I need to do?"

"Just check on the sheep. They are off the fields ready for me to start the shearing tomorrow. Your chicks and ducklings are still all there. Have fun with your day. When is Mac due?"

"Later this afternoon."

"I'll start shearing tomorrow. It doesn't seem to be getting any cooler."

"Ok. Now go." She shooed him out of the kitchen, "and I'll have a name by the time you get back."

He enjoyed the sun at his back as he rode across the valley to the family farm to pick up May. The day was promising to turn into a rare glorious one and it would be even more so with his sister.

As he pulled into the yard May ran out of the house, alerted to his arrival by the dogs. He pulled off his helmet as his mother appeared as well. She gave her younger son a wave from the doorway as she threw the tea-towel over her shoulder. The dogs milled around her, knowing it was their breakfast time.

With May now by his side he asked, "the hills or a beach?"

"The beach. I fancy a dabble in the sea." May smiled at him, excited to be going out with her brother.

"All right. We'll head to the peninsular and see if we can find a quiet one." He got May's helmet out of the bike's side-bags.

"Enjoy yourselves. You going to stay for dinner George love?" Hester asked in Welsh from the door step.

"Course I can." He crossed over to his mother and gave her a hug.

"That is lovely. Take care."

"We will."

She gave his arm a motherly squeeze. He looked down into her face and saw the concern written across it.

"I am fine ma, really."

"But you haven't talked about it. You still aren't quite my little boy again. We all still skirt around it."

"We all cope in different ways. Truly I am fine. It has changed me but not that much. It was my choice to go." He tried to reassure his mother again but she still didn't believe him. She was convinced that nearly dying must have affected him as much as it had May. She knew that even though they were close the twins still hadn't talked about what had happened between themselves. May had found it easier to talk to Davy Rhys about it all. She was glad May had got together with Davy as he was a good young man and all he wanted to do was love her. With a sigh she returned to the kitchen once the twins had left.

They travelled along roads that got smaller and smaller till they reached a car park that looked over the small island of Bardsey. George pulled out an OS map and they found a path leading to a secluded beach, "shall we try this one?"

"Looks good. What did you bring for food?"

"You'll have to wait and see. Grab the picnic blanket and I'll bring the bags."

"I like surprises." She laughed.

"I know you do." He studied her for a moment, had some of the weight of guilt lifted from her. He hadn't seen her for a few weeks.

He watched as she ran ahead with the map in one hand and the picnic blanket rolled under her arm. She turned and the sun caught her face making it radiate with happiness. Today would be a day free from worries.

She was like a little girl when she pulled off her own biker leathers revealing a pair of shorts. She dragged him down to the sea and with a squeal jumped into the surf. He rolled up his jeans and wiggled his toes. It was lovely to feel the damp warm sand between his toes. She called out, "come on."

"I'm coming." He was glad he had brought on a whim a child's bucket and spade though she didn't know it yet. As he stepped into the chilly water she grabbed his hand, "this is lovely isn't it? Better then working."

"Glad to hear it." He smiled.

"I have good news." She said as she let the water wash around her ankles.

"Go on."

"You are looking at a qualified teacher."
He hugged her, "that is brilliant."

"I've started applying for jobs but might have to be a sub for a while."   "That's better than nothing." He remarked as they walked back up the beach to the shade under the cliffs.

"What about you?"

"What about me?"

"Lily lets you pretty much run the farm. What about seeing if she'll let you breed some of the sheep you've always wanted."

"The Balwens?"

"Them. There's no harm asking is there?" She remarked as she spread the blanket.

"Very true." George replied thoughtful as he opened his saddlebags.

"So what do we have for food?"

"Well, first, I'd thought you might like this." He pulled out the child's bucket shaped like a castle and a spade in a matching yellow.
May squealed with delight, "you silly man, but my silly man." She took the held out bucket and spade. Only her brother would get her something so silly and sweet all at the same time. He knew her too well. He obviously knew she would pick the beach but she knew he preferred the mountains, so different but so alike.

They lay on the blanket after eating their full of butter smothered Bara Birth, ham and tomato chutney sandwiches plus cheese and crackers. For drinks there was a bottle of sharp homemade lemonade and a bottle of water. Some of the cheese had been some of Lily's attempt at making cheese. May was pleasantly surprised, "this isn't bad."

"Definitely better then her first two batches. I wasn't allow out unless I brought some of this with me. She may not be able to cook but she sure can make cheese."

"Didn't she say she had done a course." May remarked as she ate a bit more. It tasted salty and milky like fresh feta. Teasingly she added, "perhaps it was helped by the fact it was milked with love."

"Milked with murderous intentions more like." He replied. He had not enjoyed battling with ewes resistant to being tied up and then milked with clumsy inexperienced fingers. Once he got the knack he would show Lily and then if she wanted milk she could get it herself.

George lay back on a now empty saddlebag feeling dozy while May lay with her head resting on his chest. She stared sleepily at the cliff face while trailing her fingers over the scars on his wrist, "Georgie?"

"Mmm?"

"I want you to be as happy as I am now."

"What do you mean?" He sat up on his elbows to better see his sister's face. She turned her face to look at him, "find yourself someone to be with. I don't want you to end up lonely."

"I'm all right. Don't go setting me up on any blind dates. Anyway, what brought this on?" He reached over and brushed a strand of hair off her face.

"I have a confession to make. Me and Davy have been seeing each other." She looked away, afraid how he would react.

"Finally." George grinned, "it took him long enough. Why didn't you tell me earlier?" He had felt that May was happier than ever and had wondered why.

"What? You kept telling him not to go near me." She protested, "he respects you too much which is why it took him so long."

"When did you get together?"

"We sort of agreed to give it a go at the party." She shifted uncomfortably; this wasn't how she thought George would react, "and the other thing is we are now engaged."

"Wow, that was fast? Are you sure you are doing the right thing?" He looked at her with concern.

"This isn't me reacting to Duncan." She reassured him, "this is me, the me I once was and the most you'll get of that me back."

"What about you wanting to leave here?"

"He said he will go wherever I go. He's a mechanic so can pretty much get a job anywhere."

"If you are sure of it all then I am happy for you." He smiled softly. "Thank you, it means a lot." She took his hand and pushed her fingers between his, "I've told him everything. He came with me when I went to see the therapist."

"Oh." He sat up. This had become serious, "how did it go?"

"Good. It felt good to finally talk to someone else about it and it's not like he is a stranger so I was comfortable about doing it. It was still scary." She studied his hand. She glanced up, "I so should have listened to all of you but I didn't want to. I had convinced myself that it was because none of you understood him and only I did. I thought I loved him.

Like George and the girls, May attracted the boys. Unlike her twin she was outgoing enough to date any that dared ask her out. Duncan was a few years older than her but remembered her from school. He had bumped into her on a night out and had fallen for her smile. He invited her out. She had discovered him to be a gentleman and a bit cheeky. Before she knew it she had moved in with him after only seeing him for a few months. At first she didn't notice he was starting to isolate her from friends and family. He was only a labourer and part time farm hand and she had an evening job so had thought nothing of it.

Then she found herself ringing in sick for her course and job and then she stopped going. He began to undermine her brightness as if he was jealous of it. He started to tame her free spirit with criticisms and she became a prisoner in his flat. At first she didn't mind, it was nice to have a man who didn't want her to work but then he started to hit her, just occasionally and not too hard that others would see, "he would always apologise and promise not to do it again and that he would get help. He would say it was him and nothing I was doing though it was always something I had said or done that provoked him. I thought the baby would calm him."

"You don't have to say any of this." He tried to stop her. She may want to talk about it but he didn't want to.

"I do, I do. When he started to hurt you I could feel it."

"I knew he was hurting you too." He remembered one time when he felt his legs begin to buckle beneath him while he was at a sheepdog trial late in the season. He had clutched hard to his crook to stop himself dropping to the ground. He knew then something had happened to his sister but didn't know what at the time.

"If you had died I wanted to die with you." She gulped back a sob. She remembered seeing George pale apart from the black bruises lying in the hospital bed attached to machines and drips. She squeezed her eyes shut to try and get rid of the image. He gathered her up in his arms and held her close. He buried his face in her hair to hide his own tears. He didn't like seeing her so upset.

"We knew something was truly amiss at Christmas. I came to get you but he wouldn't let me see you. We didn't even know you were pregnant. We couldn't understand why you were shunning all of us."

It was a Christmas that they didn't want to remember, even more so then when their father had died. Their mother had kept glancing out of the windows hoping to see May arrive with a car loaded with the presents she always bought far too many of. Even George was worried as May hadn't spoken to him for several weeks. He had her friends ringing up in concern as well. Albert remarked as he entered the kitchen, "maybe she is eating with Duncan first."

"But she would have told us." Their mother replied.

"I'll go and fetch her. Maybe her car has broken down." George offered.

"Take care in the snow." Hester said with a frown of worry. She wrung the tea-towel in her hand. Her daughter had appeared to have become a recluse. She had barely spoken to her in the last two months and she missed her daughter's easy conversations.

Down in Caernorfon George glanced up at the window of the flat but couldn't see anyone. Had they gone out? He approached the door into the building and pressed the buzzer. No one checked who he was as the door lock clicked to let him in.

He could hear the TV loud through the door as he knocked. He heard swearing inside, "who the fuck would be here on Christmas Day? I hope you haven't invited your family over?"
There was an indiscernible murmured reply.

"Maybe they'll go away. Take the hint and bugger off."   "Duncan." May warned cautiously.

"Fine. If they want money they won't get any." Duncan stomped across the flat to the door. He peered through the spyhole and rolled his eyes. Why would they not leave him and May alone? He pulled the door open and glared at George and demanded, "what do you want?"

"I'm here to fetch May."

"No you aren't."

"Why not?"

Duncan shrugged his shoulders. He didn't have to give a reason to George.

"Come on; it's Christmas. Let her spend time with her family."

"I'm her family now. I'm all she needs."

"Can I at least see her?" George felt anger rising in him. He wanted to knock some sense into the bully before him. He was glad he was wearing his biking gloves as they were too stiff to form fists, "come on, she's my sister. May? Please?" He tried to peer round the large bulk that was Duncan but the man filled up most of the narrow gap. He spotted May looking fearfully out of the sitting room doorway. With his eyes still on her he said, "can she come over later? You are welcome as well."

"No. Bugger off!" Duncan slammed the door in George's face.

George stared at the door in shock. He was tempted to bang on the door again and force his way in except he would probably get punched in the face for it. He was probably as strong as the other but didn't feel desperate enough to risk it. He had seen May which was the important bit and she was alive and appeared unharmed. He sent a silent message to her though he knew she wouldn't hear it, "be brave. We haven't forgotten you." They had tried as children to see if they were telekinetic when they heard twins could be and had discovered they weren't.

With a heavy heart George returned to his bike. Leaning against his bike he rang home, "don't wait for me. Stick some on a plate for me and I'll eat later."

"He won't let her come?" His mother asked with a wobble in her voice. "No. I did get a glimpse of her. She seems okay. I'm going to hang around here just in case he has a change of heart or she manages to get away." "I'm so worried for her. At least you've seen her." Hester remarked with a little relief.

"So am I."

"Take care. Let us know when you are on your way back."

"Will do. Bye."

"Bye love."

He returned his phone back to his pocket and then crossed his arms to stay warm. He looked up at the flat's windows. The curtains to Duncan and May's flat were the only ones open. All the rest were closed as if their occupants had gone else where for Christmas.

May appeared at the window and he hoped she could see him; hoped she knew she was wanted whatever the bully said. He saw her put a hand on the glass but was then whipped away from the window. He saw Duncan shouting at her and she trying to stand up to him but it didn't last. He winced as he saw Duncan slap his beautiful sister round the face. He couldn't understand why May didn't dump him and get out quick. He couldn't take his eyes away from the window as May put a hand to her cheek and bowed her head.

He stayed for an hour but didn't see any more of May. Reluctantly he pulled on his helmet, turned the ignition and returned home. He wished there was something they could do. Friends and family had already tried the police but as Duncan behaved himself and May refused to say anything against him there was nothing they could do except monitor.

The tide was coming in. One half of the shell and seaweed decorated castle had already slumped. After her cry May had fallen asleep pressed against his side as if she wanted to be conjoined twins. George lay staring up at the white clouds floating across the sky. Carefully so as not to startle her he shook her awake," come on sleepy, time we made a move back. Ma will have dinner on the go."

"Mmm." She stirred and rubbed sleep and tears from her eyes as she sat up.

She looked at George and smiled, "thanks for today. It's been brilliant."

"And with a few surprises along the way."

"Don't be angry with Davy." She pleaded as she loaded up his saddlebags.

"I'm not. I really am pleased for both of you." He replied once he had stood and stretched. He took the bottle of water offered and drank it dry, "surprised but happy."

She grinned, "I do so love you Georgie Porgie." She declared with a huge May grin. In return she got his small affectionate smile, their mother's smile.

The dogs announced the wanderers' return and Hester stepped out on to the back porch to greet them, "have a good day?"

"Definitely Ma." May declared as she embraced her mother, "we went for a paddle in the sea, built a sandcastle, ate and drank. Talked."   "And did you tell him?" She whispered.

May nodded with a big smile and then asked, "is he here?"

"How did your brother take it?"

May ran into the farmhouse, "Davy? Davy, it's safe. He won't kill you." From the top of the stairs Davy announced, "thank God for that. I don't think I could have coped knowing you were all enjoying Hester's food." He tentatively walked downstairs, glancing through the banister to see if he could see George.

George gave his mother a hug as he entered the house. She gave him a kiss on the cheek, "how are you?"

"You don't need to worry. I'm not going to harm him." She sighed with relief.

"Hang on, did you all know?" She nodded as he walked in and demanded, "May?! Why am I the last to know?" He found her at the bottom of the stairs holding Davy's hand, "oh, hello?"

"Err, hello?" Davy said cautiously, "I'm sorry I didn't tell you."

"It's all right. I forgive you. You've made May happy which is the important thing."

"I am serious about it all Georgie. We aren't going to get married straight away. I wanted to show May that I wasn't ever going to hurt her."

"Come on, time to celebrate." May laughed as she led the two most important men in her life into the dining room.

Dinner went long into the evening with much laughter. George ended up staying the night in his old room that was now Albert's eldest's room with the boy on the floor. He'd drunk too much and was soon out for the count. It had been a great night and he really was happy for May and Davy. Now he understood why she wanted him to find a girlfriend. Did he dare let her set him up on a few dates?

10

In the morning George was slow to wake up until he remembered he needed to start shearing. He stumbled out of bed, just remembering his nephew was on the floor, except the sleeping bag was empty as the boy was already up.

He ran down the stairs and out to his bike.

Hearing the noise May staggered out of bed herself and wrapped a bed sheet around her. She opened the window as she heard her brother's Triumph start. She leant out of the window and called out, "you off without saying bye?" George looked up as he was about to put his helmet on. He waved. Davy appeared at May's side and leant on the sill and remarked teasingly, "no rest for the wicked." He gave May's bum a squeeze and she squealed and then hissed,

"he's watching."

"I'm just making him jealous." Davy teased.

"I can see you Davy Rhys." George called out, "I'll get you back soon, when you least expect it."

"I'm shaking." Davy laughed as he pulled May from the window and she went willingly with a giggle.

George rolled his eyes but smiled as he pulled on his helmet. Back to work he went.

By the time Lily and Mac woke up George was on his third sheep after having got changed. The day was rapidly warming up and becoming muggy. Lily took her farm manager a cold drink after sorting out breakfast for her late rising guests. Mac was in the shower. She leant over the pen and waited for George to finish shearing the encumbered ewe. The three dogs limply wagged their tails in greeting in the shade of the barn.

As the sheep trotted off with a shake of its head George stretched his stiff back. He heard a cough and turned to see Lily watching. He blushed as he saw her staring at him. She wondered why he hadn't become a model considering his looks. All he was wearing were a pair of torn old jeans and a vest top that had briefly ridden up until he pulled it back down, hiding the scar he was still uncomfortable about, and his toned tanned body from farm work. He wore his battered leather wide brimmed hat and sunglasses.

She silently held out the large glass of water as she wasn't sure she would make sense if she spoke. He smiled at her as he took it, "cheers."
She watched as he drank it down. She began thinking she was in some Diet Coke advert. All it needed was him to take his top of. Would a Diet Coke ad manage to make sheep shearing sexy? She came back to real life when he handed back the glass. Their hands touched and she felt what felt like a shock of electricity go through her.

She jumped and blushed with guilt when she heard footsteps behind her. She turned and forced a smile when she saw Mac in his landowner outfit of checked shirt and jeans and wide brimmed hat which didn't suit him. It looked so much better on George she considered and glanced back at George as he wrangled another ewe. Yeap, definitely better looking. Mac was too pale and thin. Mac looked suspiciously between the two of them- had something been going on while he was in London?

They were all distracted by the arrival of a car and Davy got out and greeted Lily with a wave. He wandered down and as George finished another ewe he said in Welsh, "I've come to help."
"You mean May has sent you."

Davy laughed, "you got me. May sent me. Is this it? Mr Lewis really did get rid of a lot of sheep. Who's the oddball?"

"Lily's boyfriend."

"Aah." Davy warily eyed the man as Mac eyed him back suspiciously.

"Hi Davy, want a drink? You here to help?" Lily asked brightly.

"Yeah. I'm here to help and no to the drink for the moment but thanks." Davy replied as he found a spare plug socket and set up his borrowed shears. He twisted his baseball cap round to protect the back of his neck before grabbing a sheep and rolling it on to its back. Gripping it between his legs he began shearing, the skill coming back to him quickly.

Lily left the men to it as she went to see her guests off and make some sandwiches for lunch. Mac leant against the pen as if he owned the place. Davy raised an eyebrow at George in question. George shrugged and muttered in Welsh, "ignore him."

Mac let the men carry on with the shearing for a little while as he tried to decide if there was anything going on between Lily and the welshman. He had checked him out back in London with his mate from the MET. They hadn't found any criminal records but they had found a victim statement which was more intriguing. His mate wouldn't reveal the contents which was frustrating as it meant he had to do some investigating of his own. He had the date of the statement and went rummaging through the online archives of the local paper and found a brief domestic abuse article with the defendant not given bail and that the victims had been hospitalized but were remaining anonymous. Very intriguing.

Now was his opportunity to see what more he could find out from what he believed to be one of the 'victims'. Looking at the man he couldn't believe he could have been a victim. As causal as you like Mac remarked, "I've checked up on you."

He paused to see what reaction he would get.

The friends couldn't believe how casually Mac had made the comment.

Davy opened his mouth but shut it again when he saw his friend shake his head.

Behind his sunglasses George rolled his eyes. Prick!

"I thought I'd best check as you know how scatter-brained Lily can be. Had to check there wasn't a psycho living with my girl." Mac ignored the fact Lily knew how to do checks as she had worked in HR before the lottery win. George knew she wasn't scatter-brained but hid his disgust at Mac's patronising tone by concentrating on shearing the ewe between his legs. He also knew she had done her own checks as nothing escaped the village grapevine.

"You'll be glad to hear I didn't find anything but I was told something else." Davy and George tried not to listen. They had a feeling they knew what was coming. Mac went on, "you may appear all macho but you aren't."

Davy couldn't let the gloating go on. He stopped shearing and demanded, "what are you trying to suggest? Do you actually know what you are talking about?" He stood up tall trying to intimidate the city-slicker and ready to defend his best friend.

"I do actually. Being beaten up by a wife beater isn't very clever." Mac sneered gleefully. Finally, a rise out of one of them.

"And where did you hear that?"

"My mate in the MET." He paused for affect, "found a victim statement and then I found an article. It was quite easy to put two and two together." "You think so? You don't know the half of it so don't go accusing me of anything." George angrily declared, surprising both Mac and Davy. His nails dug into his palms as he approached

Mac now that the sheep he had been shearing was done. Mac actually took a step back as he saw the muscles in George's arms tense. Yes, he had wanted to provoke George as an excuse to get Lily to get rid of him but he was still surprised it might happen. He closed his eyes and braced himself for a fist hitting his jaw.

Just as he thought it wasn't coming it came. His head snapped round. As he turned, shifting his jaw to check it hadn't been dislocated he was astonished to find Davy in his personal space and not George. Davy hissed in warning, "do not talk of things you don't understand otherwise I'll hit you again."

Mac, in shock, nodded and turned as if to go. Davy grabbed his arm, "you aren't going anywhere yet."

Mac looked in the direction Davy was looking and saw George walking away, his shoulders tensed and hunched. Once George had left the yard Davy let Mac go and as if nothing had happened calmly climbed back into the pen and grabbed another ewe to shear.

Angrily Mac stalked off, back to the house. He was glad neither Lily nor his friends had been there to see him nearly wet himself and he would never admit it if asked. But now, thanks to the friend, he would get Lily to sack George and then maybe she would give up on the farming idea and come back to London. He wanted her back. It was boring and lonely without her. One night stands were alright but they only filled the sex space, not the fun space. Thankfully Lily didn't seem to be aware of those even though one of them had been Claire. In fact he had met up with the blonde slut a few times for the fun.

He composed himself before walking into the kitchen. He rubbed at his jaw, that man had certainly given it a good thump. Lily glanced up as he entered but then turned to look at him with concern, "what happened?"

"You need to sack your labourer. He has dangerous friends. That mate of his hit me and he would have as well if I didn't hit him first."

"Why on earth?!"

"All I said to him was that I had done a criminal check on him."

"Why would you do that?" She frowned.

"Because you probably didn't."

"Umm, yes I did Mac." She corrected with indignation, "and he has no record."

"Did you know he got in a fight?" He pursued.

"No?" She answered cautiously. She wasn't sure where Mac was going with this. She wanted to see George to get his side. She had never seen George angry so Mac wasn't telling her something.

"Yes. He's violent Lily. I don't want him working for you anymore." He saw a look cross her face and jumped straight in with his next plea before she stopped being confused, "sell this place and come back to London." She was shocked, "what?"

"Come on. You know you can't do this. You'll always be an outsider here. Come back to London to be with me and your friends."

"You are so wrong Mac McGuire." She exploded, "you've never understood and you never will. I don't want to go back to London. I love it here." "You won't when you get snowed in." He retorted.

"Then I'll get through it." She declared angrily, "and I did all the correct checks. I made sure he had no criminal records that I needed to know about and I checked out his references as well. I know there is a gap in his employment but I wasn't worried. And, in all honesty, you probably deserved to be hit. You like provoking others."

"I'm not staying if you are going to be like this." He shouted. He so wanted to throw something. He grabbed a plate from the draining board and threw it at the floor.

"Fine! Go then! See if I care. I'm not going anywhere."
She stood her ground. She wasn't going to back down. She
wasn't going to simper and she didn't want make-up sex.
She wanted Mac to see she was no longer going to always
roll over for him. She was made of stronger stuff now.

He wasn't going to back down either. He found his
keys, phone and wallet on a kitchen shelf and grabbed
them. He stomped out of the house, got in his car, slammed
the door shut and with some heavy revving drove up the
track and away.

Inside Lily sank to the floor gasping for breath.
What had she done? Had she lost Mac? Did she actually
still want Mac? Their lives were poles apart now, could
their relationship stay alive. Guilt began to creep in as she
started to feel relieved that he was gone. No one, not even
Mac, was going to stop her from what she had always
wanted to do. Then she realised she didn't know what had
happened to her two new friends.

Ignoring the broken plate on the floor she ran out of
the house and across the yard. The dogs jumped up at the
sight of her running. She was stopped by the fencing and
shouted, "Davy?"
He glanced behind and then returned to shearing.
Impatiently Lily waited for him to finish. When he let the
ewe go she tried again, "Davy?"
He didn't care how rude he was about Mac, "was that
the shit leaving?"
She was thrown by his coarse language. What had
been said out here? Cautiously she answered, "yes?
We've just had a big argument. Davy, where is
George? What happened out here?"
  "George will be back when he's ready to come back."
  "What's that suppose to mean?"
  "Look Lily, I like you, but your boyfriend is an arse
hole. He was trying to pick a fight with George. I can't

control myself as well as him so I thumped your boyfriend."

"What did he say?"

"He insinuated that my best friend let himself get beaten up." He crossed the pen to stand opposite Lily. He sighed, "look, I think there is something you need to know."

"What? She asked, suddenly afraid.

"You didn't hear this from me alright?" She nodded

"Yes he was beaten but he was trying to rescue his sister."

"Oh." She didn't know what to say to that, "oh." She grabbed the rail, "wow… is that…? His wrist…? His side…?" Davy nodded.

"Is he going to be alright on his own?"

"He'll be fine." He reassured her, "I'll get these sheep finished off for you."

"Thanks."

The afternoon got muggier and black clouds loomed over the other side of the hill. Lily glanced with concern at the clouds and then into the yard.
George still hadn't reappeared.

Davy had finished shearing and had stuffed the fleeces into a couple of large Hessian sacks for her. He started to feel worried himself as he glanced at his watch and at the clouds as the wind started to pick up. At his feet Lou whined. As much to reassure himself as well as the collie he commented, "he'll be back."

Though he wanted to stay till George got back he needed to get off home and help his father for an hour to two in the garage. As he left he said to Lily, "send me a text when he gets back."
She nodded.

The thunderstorm finally arrived and with it came the rain. The dogs hid under the table as the thunder rolled over and the lightening streaked across the sky. It had been building for several days. She put the porch light on so George could find his way back until with a crash of thunder and lightening the lights went out. She swore to herself before fumbling around in the poor light to find a torch or matches or candles, anything to create light.

Stan barked and though he was scared by the thunder a more powerful instinct drew him to the front door. It opened and closed. Lily froze where she was and then called out, "George?"

"Sorry."

She hurried into the hallway where he stood dripping wet and shivering as he awkwardly pulling off his boots. She asked, "what happened?"

"I found myself walking and walking and before I knew it I was a bit lost till I worked out where I was. Is he here?"

"You should have called." She protested, "and no Mac isn't. He's gone. We had a big fight. Come on, let's get you into a hot bath and warm you up. Do you want anything to eat or drink?"

"No thanks."

He let her guide him up to her bathroom where she set the water running and lit a pile of candles before turning to his wet clothes. She wondered what was going on in his mind as he looked dazed and numb. He didn't protest as she pulled down his jeans. She went to pull his vest off but he pushed her hands away. Gently she took them off where he held his top down, "it's all right I kind of know. Davy told me."

"How much?" He whispered.

"Just enough to understand now why everyone has been so protective over you and May." She pulled the vest off and guided him into the bath, "from what Davy has told me about what Mac said I wouldn't have stopped you hitting him. I probably would have hit him myself. Mac is an idiot sometimes." She dipped the flannel in the hot water George had gingerly lowered himself into. She wrung it over his chilly back and ignored the desire she felt between her thighs. She went on, "he likes to provoke people so he can have a good argument or debate about politics and money. I don't think he was expecting a violent reaction when Davy hit him. I'm sorry about Mac."

She wrung the flannel over his back again when he shuddered, "George?" Looking round she saw him bury his face in his hands as he tried not to sob.

Ignoring the fact he was wet she hugged him over the bath, "ssh, it's all right. Do you know, I think your friends are amazing. They care so much for you. I don't think mine do." She sighed. None of them had rung her recently and in all honesty she hadn't rung them either. That all now felt like part of another life. She felt sure Hillside Farm was where she was meant to belong.

She gently rocked George, amazed she had such compassion within herself, until the sobs stopped racking his body. She wondered if he had fallen asleep until he spoke into her chest, "sorry. I don't know where that came from."

"I think you needed it."

He broke out of her embrace, "do you have any alcohol?"

"I haven't finished the wine me and Mac started last night. Do you want some?"

"Please."

It didn't take her long to bring the half empty bottle of red wine up with two glasses. She poured it into one and handed it to George, who although red eyed, seemed to have recovered his composure. Now he was enjoying the hot water and it soothed his aching feet, legs and shoulders. He felt some of his woes melting away. With the glass in his hand he asked, "the power not coming back on yet?"

"No."

"Have you checked the fuse box?"

"No? Should I?"

"We'll do it in a bit. Sorry I disappeared on you and Davy. I just needed to get away before I did something I would regret."

"I'm just glad you are safe."

As he finished the wine he asked, "any chance of a towel?"

"Oh, of course." She put her own glass down and went to find a towel.

She handed it over as he climbed out of the bath and sat down beside her.

He asked, "any left?"

"A little bit." She poured the last into his glass, "feeling better?"

"A lot thanks. I think this will count as one of the odder places to hang out during a thunderstorm." He remarked cheerfully, the wine already going to his head from an empty stomach.

"Definitely." She agreed.

Neither could recall who made the first move but one minute they were sitting next to each other, the next they were kissing. Lily couldn't believe how good his lips felt. After all those day dreams she now knew what it was like to kiss George. Heavenly.

She didn't stop his hands from disappearing up the back of her strappy top and found her braless as she straddled him. She pressed herself against him and he could feel her firm breasts pressing against his chest and he ached for her. His hands moved down under her waistband where he gave her a bum a squeeze as she nuzzled his neck with little moans of pleasure.

She stood and quickly pulled off her shorts and knickers. George pulled off his wet boxers before drawing her back down. She willingly straggled him and kissed him as she let him enter her, he grabbed her hips.

They lay beside each other afterwards. Neither of them said anything for a moment as they tried to recover their composure. What had they done? Lily rolled on to her side. She didn't want the moment to be spoilt. It had been the best sex she had had in a while. She took his right wrist in her hand and ran her fingers over the scars. She glanced into George's face to see how he reacted. He watched her dreamily in the candlelight. Seeing the question in her face he remarked, "my bones are held together with metal plates now." Silently she ran her fingers over the long scar on his right side.

"Repairing the damage to my kidney."

Suddenly he sat up taking her by surprise. He grabbed the towel that had been abandoned and wrapped it round himself as the lights flickered back on in her bedroom. He softly remarked, "I should go."

She gulped. The moment was now gone, "you don't have to."

"I do."

She watched him leave and heard him call his two dogs to him. She hugged herself. What were they going to do now? Would she confess to Mac or would she dump the man? Would she and George now awkwardly skirt around each other? She spotted George's second glass of wine and downed the last of it.

11

George was already up, probably making more noise then was necessary in the kitchen, when Lily woke up. Memories of the night before came back to her and she realised she didn't regret what had happened. She wrapped her dressing gown around herself before venturing downstairs. She hung in the doorway as he moved around the kitchen.

Feeling eyes on him he turned. She gave him a shy smile. "Last night?"

"I don't regret it." She admitted.

"Oh." He was taken aback by that answer, "actually, neither do I."

"Good."

"What about Mac?"

"I'll deal with him."

"Umm. Look, last night… I think my hand has kind of been forced." He turned away from looking at Lily.

She walked into the kitchen and with a frown asked, "what do you mean?"

"I'll tell you everything but I don't want to do it here. Can we go for a walk?"

"Let me go get dressed."

With the dogs running ahead they began walking through the fields. They walked in silence; Lily waited for George to start talking in his own time.

May was three months pregnant though she had told no one about it. In what felt like a different life everyone would have know by now and be excited for her. She hadn't as yet dared tell Duncan as she didn't know how he would react. She hoped that with it would come some freedom again and the chance to see her family. The only time she was allowed out was when he chose to let her. There were still the occasional moments when he became the Duncan she first met and he would take her out for a meal.

She had hoped he would let her see her family for Christmas but when she suggested it he threatened to take her phone away, her only access to the outside world, not that she dared use it much.

On Christmas Day she impatiently made their dinner. She looked at the chicken and roast potatoes and carrots and thought it made a measly meal compared to the feast her family would be having. She looked at her little Christmas tree and though she had decorated it with love and care it still looked sad. Hidden in a box buried under bedding were small presents for everyone that she had snuck into the shopping. Under the drooping tree were four presents, two for her and two for Duncan.

He went to see his own family with a box of presents for them wrapped by her. She had contemplated slipping out but found he had locked the door and taken all the keys.

He had returned and they had eaten lunch. She had sat in silence while he had told her about how his family had liked their presents. After dinner he had retreated to the TV while she had cleared up.

Her hopes were raised when Duncan answered the door and she heard her brother trying to negotiate with her boyfriend. She peered out into the hallway hoping to see George and make herself feel that she could keep going. She wanted to get his tiny present and give it to him but she didn't want to reveal her hidden presents to Duncan. She caught a brief glimpse of George and then Duncan slammed the door shut. Duncan muttered, "thinks he's better then me. No one's better than me. Your place is here with me May."

"Yes Duncan." She answered as she watched him settle back on to his spot on the sofa. Slowly she moved round to the window to look out. She saw George on the phone and then look up. Duncan called from the sofa, "come and sit down."

She didn't respond and he turned in his seat to see what she was doing. He rolled his eyes and got up. He grabbed her hand away from the window, "come and sit down."

She turned on him, "no. I'm not doing anything wrong, just looking at the snow."

"You rang him didn't you?" He accused her.

"No I didn't." She protested.

"Liar."

"I'm not lying. You can check my phone and the house phone. Nothing."

"Don't lie to me. Don't push me."

"I'm telling you the truth." She protested again.

He slapped her face and then returned to his seat. He ordered, "sit down." She blinked the tears away and tried to rub the stinging away. She didn't want to push him any further and sat down. He pulled her closer and put his arm round her and remarked cheerfully, "isn't this nice." She gave him a tight smile.

After Christmas Day he had been lovely to her. They had gone for a nice walk and then lunch at a pub. She decided now was the time to tell Duncan about their baby growing inside of her. If she told him she hoped the new year might be better. She made him lunch on New Year's Eve and then told him at the table, "I have a surprise to tell you about."

"A surprise?"

"You're going to be a daddy." She grinned.

His face lost all its colour and he demanded, "you're what?!"

Her smile disappeared. That hadn't been the reaction she was expecting. She whispered, "I'm pregnant."

He stood. He had a murderous look on him.

She leapt up, knocking her chair over and fled to the bathroom. She flung the door shut and bolted it. With shaking hands she pulled out her phone and sent a single worded text to George: "HELP"

Duncan rattled the handle and banged on the door. He roared, "May, get out here!

She stepped away from the door as she saw it shudder as Duncan threw his weight against it. The bolt protested. With another thrust from Duncan the door sprung open, the bolt bent. She huddled against the back wall of the bathroom. He grabbed her and pulled her out. He threw her to the floor. Towering over her he shouted, "you are not pregnant!"

"I am." She said to the floor. She pleaded, "please don't hurt me Duncan, please don't."

"You are a whore. A manipulative whore who wants my money." He kicked her in the stomach.

"I don't want your money."

"Why did you get pregnant then?" He demanded as he kicked her again, ignoring the fact he hadn't let her get her contraceptive pill prescription renewed.

"I thought you wanted a family like your sister has." She whimpered.

"I decide that, not you." He spat as he grabbed her hair and pulled her up on to her knees. He thumped her and blood began to ooze from her nose. With a booted foot he pushed her up against the wall. She tried to clutch her stomach as she felt pain shoot through it.

George was waiting for a text from Bugsy while giving his sister's pony a brush. Bugsy was trying to sort tickets for a New Year's party in Bangor through his contacts there. When his phone went he eagerly pulled it out. He stared in surprise at who it was. With trepidation he opened it. The one word text was enough for him to abandon May's pony and run for his bike.

He rode as fast as he dared and skidded to a stop outside the block of flats. He ran up the stairs after pressing every bell till someone released the door. He stumbled on them as it felt like he had been punched in the stomach. It briefly took his breath away. He staggered up and made it to the top of the stairs.

A neighbour peered out of the door. He had been expecting a policeman.

He remarked, "I've called the police."

George ignored him and ran to the flat door. He tried the handle and was surprised to find it unlocked. He ran in, "May?"

He found her against the wall of the sitting room in a growing pool of blood. He crouched beside her, "bastard. Where is he May?"

She opened her eyes at her brother's voice and then they widened. Seeing it

George stood and turned but was too slow to react. He was unbalanced by Duncan's blood lust filled swing now fuelled with whisky as well, the bottle in his hand. George staggered and fell, hitting his head on the corner of the coffee table.

He raised his head feeling dazed. He tried to get up but Duncan stamped down on his wrist and hand. George cried out. Duncan bent down, "how dare you enter my home uninvited."

"May..." George said through gritted teeth.

"Come to play the hero have you? Come to rescue your slut of a sister." Duncan sneered as he ground the heel of his boot into George's wrist. George moaned and winced as he felt bones break. Duncan added, "what I do in my home is my own concern."

"May..."

"You can't rescue her." Duncan laughed and he kicked George in the back. George grunted in pain.

"Don't." May cried out weekly.

"Well, you shouldn't have got pregnant then." Duncan was just spurred on and he continued to kick George even as he tried to get up and out of the way. As George looked like he might actually get up Duncan stamped down on the man's wrist again, "oh no you don't."
George slumped down. He looked over at May. He had come to rescue her and was failing.

There was the sound of sirens but Duncan didn't care. He was enjoying himself too much. He hadn't had a good fight for a while and he was loving the fact he was in control of it. He didn't care it was a one sided fight,

Two burly policeman grabbed Duncan from behind by his arms. He fought them, swinging the bottle at them. They twisted the bottle out of his hand and pulled him away from George's still body. He laughed as he gave George a final kick, catching his ankle. Another pair showed up and helped push Duncan up against the wall and handcuffed him. Another ambulance was called.

Now it was safe for them the first pair of paramedics stepped in. They split up to attend to each twin. The woman crouched beside May, "you're safe now lovey. What are your names?"

"May." May whispered, "and he's my brother George." She watched wide eyed as the other paramedic checked her brother.

"May? Look at me. I need to check you over." The paramedic said softly. May turned her head to look at the paramedic.

"Where has he hurt you?"
May looked down and saw the blood. She began crying in shock, "I've lost the baby."

"How far a long were you?"

"Three months."

"All right. How is he Clive?" She looked at her partner.

"Not good. He's taken quite a beating."

"Ok. May?"

May sniffed as she tried to get her emotions under control. She needed to be strong for George now.

"Once the other ambulance has arrived we are going to take George first." She nodded.

"Do you understand?"

"Yes." May whispered with fear, "don't let him die."

"We won't. I've got to help my partner for a moment and then I'll be back over. Ok?"

"Okay."

By the time Hester Risoll with Albert arrived May was cleaned up and the miscarriage confirmed. She should have felt grateful that the baby had saved her from worst damage from the beating but she didn't. She lay in a cubicle hugging a pillow with fear. The ache in her back was put down to the miscarriage though she felt sure she was feeling her twin's pain. The loss of the baby she could accept but she didn't want to think what would happen is she lost her brother. She had watched George get taken away with a splint on his wrist, a bandage on his head and lying on a spinal board. She hadn't been far behind.

At the sight of her mother May burst into new tears. Hester wrapped her daughter up in her loving arms. She was relieved to see her daughter safe and not as badly harmed as she feared. Letting her daughter go Hester asked, "where's George?"

"I don't know." May hiccuped, "I haven't seen him since I got here."

"I'll go and find out." Albert said, "you stay here ma."

He returned shortly with a solemn faced doctor. Hester sat on the bed and wrapped an arm round her daughter. Albert stood in a corner with a frown. The doctor cleared her throat, "I'm sorry no one has come and seen you. We have been working on your son. He's just been sent to theatre." "Theatre?" Hester asked fearfully.

"His right kidney was damaged by the kicking he got. Also his wrist bones are going to need to be held together with a metal plate."

"Oh?"

"He also has a few broken ribs, a bruised spine and possibly concussion."

"Oh." Hester tried to stay strong but she could feel the tears rolling.

In his corner Albert sank to the floor in shock. May clung to her mother.

"As soon as he's out we'll know more."

"And my daughter?" Hester carefully asked.

The doctor picked up the notes and glanced over them, "she's to stay overnight and unless something crops up she'll be free to go tomorrow."

12

Lily and George sat on a rock looking across the valley. He held his scarred wrist in his other hand as he waited for Lily's reaction. Lou's head rested on his knee. She didn't say anything but she did take his right hand. She kissed the scars.

"I hope I'm not about to get sympathy sex." He teased to break the tense silence.

Lily looked into his face, "you've been through a lot then."

"I'm fine. Come on, we'd best get back." He stood. Now it had been told he didn't want to talk about it.

Two weeks in hospital had been more than enough followed by several outpatient appointments to ensure his kidney hadn't developed permanent damage. He hadn't enjoyed lying in a hospital bed covered with boot shaped bruises and aching all over. If that wasn't enough the police had visited for a statement and to take photos and ask permission for his medical records as evidence.

He had come round to a doctor's face and had only understood half of what was said to him. He had been more relieved to see May before she was discharged. Her eyes were red rimmed still and she looked tired but he could see she was resisting the urge to throw herself on him. She had held his hand and they had sat in a companionable silence that she had missed. After a bit he had asked, "are you okay?"

"A lot better then you." She teased.

"Haha. So much for appreciating me coming to rescue you."

"I do Georgie, I do. I've missed you." She squeezed his hand, "I'll be back tomorrow all right?"

Walking back through the fields Lily sought out George's hand. It felt right when he let her take it. They didn't say anything about what they were doing.

The romantic idyll was disturbed by a very large bouquet of roses on the back porch. Lily sighed. It was Mac trying to apologise. She was sure of it as she bent down to find the little card. Written inside in the florist's handwriting was:

'Forgive me? Mac.'

George looked over her shoulder, "mmm. I think you are going to need to decide who you want to be with. I don't want to be your bit on the side." "You make a very nice bit on the side." She teased and stuck her tongue out at him but he wasn't playing. He frowned at her, "I mean it. Yes I fancy you like mad but I still have a sensible head on."
She blushed. Did she dare tell him how much she fancied him too? She couldn't believe she was thinking it as she asked herself- why can't I have both? Men do it all the time. Her thoughts were interrupted by George remarking, "I'll leave you to decide who its going to be. Let me know when you have decided."

"You aren't going to keep away are you?"

"No. Just no sex or talk of it. Ok?"
She nodded, "ok." Then an image of him last night flashed into her mind and she couldn't help smiling.
He rolled his eyes before saying, "I've got a wall to finish."

"What about lunch?"

"I'm not hungry." He lied, "Stan, Lou, Bea, come."
The dogs ran ahead as he headed back into the fields via the yard for some tools.

Lily watched him go with growing frustration. Damn Mac. Did she still love him? Was she just lusting after George as she didn't have Mac? This was obviously what she had to decide. She decided to put it off for another day. This was the sort of thing she would talk to the girls about but they weren't around and it would be unfair to talk it over with May considering her brother was part of the issue. The men could fester and think what they wanted to think while she decided. This was unfair. George had put her on the spot.

The thoughts kept going round her head and she swore as she stomped into the house, abandoning the roses. She never really liked roses anyway. She began wondering what flowers George would have got her instead and realised he probably didn't have a clue. There was still plenty they didn't know about each other whereas Mac was like a comfortable old jumper, an expensive comfortable old jumper.

13

Lily wasn't sure whether to be grateful or disappointed when she saw George leave the house a few evenings later all spruced up in a clean shirt and jeans. He had asked to borrow the Land Rover earlier in the day but hadn't explained why.

She hoped he was meeting up with friends but another part of her wondered if he was going out on a date. He had mentioned in the past that May had been trying to set him up, and maybe now he had finally let her. She felt a little jealous of whoever he was meeting up with ignoring the fact she had Mac, though she didn't know if she still wanted to be with him.

George didn't tell her because he wasn't sure of his feelings on the matter. He knew he couldn't rely on Lily to give Mac up so he needed to find someone of his own. He was nervous as he parked in the main square of Caernafon and then walked to the Italian restaurant where he was meeting May's teacher college friend. May had been thrilled to organise a date for her brother.   His thoughts kept straying to Lily and the sex they had had on the bathroom floor. He tried to put the images to one side so that he could give the woman before him a fair chance. She smiled nervously at him and tucked a
loose strand of brown hair
behind her ear, "hi."

"Hi. I'm George." He held
out his hand.

"I know who you are. I'm Caitlyn." She shifted her bag on her shoulder and he dropped his hand.

"Sorry about May doing this." He remarked as he held the door open for her.

"That's all right."

It turned into an awkward date. They talked but had nothing in common but May. They were both relieved when it came to an end. He gave her a kiss on the cheek, "it was nice meeting you but I don't think its worked out."

"That's fair. Thank you for dinner at least."

"Do you think I should let May do this again?" He asked with his small smile.

She laughed, "I don't think she's very good at matchmaking."

"Do you want to tell her or shall I?"

"I think it will come better from you. Well," she shifted uncomfortably, "I'd best go."

"Are you all right getting to your car?"

"Yeah, thanks."

He watched her walk away before heading back to the battered Land Rover. He wasn't sure whether to be relieved or not that it was over.

Lily was actually relieved when May rang inviting her on a girlie shopping trip. She needed to get away from the farm and George. He had been keeping his distance with his date as well as working with Stan and Lou on different flocks of sheep from neighbouring farms as he had managed to get into the National Sheepdog trials and everyone was keen to help him practise. She was left with Bea and practising with ducks but neither her nor the dog were interested even though George nagged her about practising. It was too hot to do anything.

She sat in the garden dozing when the phone rang. She had foolishly sat up waiting for George to come home. She reckoned that depending upon what time he came back would indicate how well the secret date had gone. The fact he wasn't early and wasn't late didn't help her worrying.

Answering the phone May declared brightly down the line, "I think you need a girlie day and leave the men playing farmer."

"I'm so glad to hear you suggest that. I was trying to do some training with Bea but neither of us were in the mood."

"Excellent. I'll be with you in half an hour and we'll go for lunch."

"See you in a bit."

May took them to Bangor and arm in arm they strolled down the main shopping area and then off down a side street to a cafe May knew. At the table while waiting for their salads May asked, "how are you finding it all?" "I know I need to build up the flock and your brother said he'll take me to Ruthvins next week to look at the stock auction."

"Has he told you of his sheep dream?"

"Sheep dream?"

"Oh he is a coward. There is a certain breed he has always liked to own. Let me see if I can find a picture." May searched online on her phone, "here we go." She turned her phone round and showed a picture of a Balwen ram with a thick dark grey fleece and a striking black and white face where the white covered most of its face. Two horns curled into backward Cs and it looked like it had white socks on. "They are bred for the Welsh mountains but that's about all I know. George knows a lot more. Anyway enough of him. I heard you had a big argument with Mac, are you alright?" She didn't mention that she hadn't liked him attacking her brother so obviously, pushing him into a corner.

Lily studied May for a moment. Did she dare talk about it? When she had spoken to Sarah over the phone all she had been told was to go for it and have a country lover and who could resist a farmer. She had expected it from Claire but not Sarah. That hadn't been the advice Lily had wanted to here. The arrival of food gave her a bit longer to decide.

For all she knew May already knew everything. How much, as twins, did they sense of each other? Finally she admitted, "yes we had an argument. It was a silly argument really."

"It didn't sound it considering Davy punched him." Lily giggled then, "oh you should have seen his face." Realising what she had just done she covered her mouth as if she could gobble the giggle back up. With wide eyes she remarked with surprise, "oh, I've just realised something."

"What?" May asked eagerly. She liked a good revelation.

"I've fallen out of love."

"Oooh, more?"

"Mac is a selfish moron. He didn't trust me to do the right checks and then he tried to start an argument with your brother and he still doesn't want me here. He wants me in London keeping him company. I don't regret my decision to come up here."

"That's good because you've made George happy." May beamed.

"What do you mean?" Lily blushed.

"You know what I mean." She hinted, "it sounds silly but its a twin thing. I know when he is really angry, sad or happy or when he is hurt. He's the same with me."

"So you knew he was angry when Mac was trying to provoke him?" May nodded and then asked, "did he get back ok? Davy said he walked away and hadn't come back by the time he left."

"Yes." Lily blushed again as she remembered the evening.

"You didn't?" May asked in disbelief.

Lily just smiled.

"Oh my God." May laughed, "I knew it, I knew it. Any good?" She cheekily asked.

"May!" Lily protested.

"Fine."

"Yes." Lily said quietly causing May to laugh again.

"So I sent him on a date for nothing."

"Was that where he was last night?"

"Yeah, but it didn't go very well." May confessed

After a few mouthfuls May became more serious, "what are you going to
do? I hope you aren't going to string my brother along."

"I'm not. He's keeping his distance until I decide." Lily answered after finishing her mouthful, "I'm going to split up with Mac."

"Yeah."

"May?"

"Mmm?" May searched for any chicken left in her salad.

"George has told me everything."

May glanced up. She didn't know how to react to that statement. She twiddled her fork with a frown.

"I think Mac forced his hand but he also looked relieved to tell me. Don't be mad at him." The excuses tumbled out of Lily's mouth, "I don't think he liked keeping it as a secret."

"It's alright. It was probably good for him." May said carefully, "he hasn't really talked about it to anyone."   "How long was he recovering?"

"Two weeks in hospital and then right up to when he came to you. He was in good health before which was apparently to his advantage." May tried to fight back the tears threatening to roll down her cheeks. She hastily brushed them away with one hand.

Lily reached for the other, "sorry. I shouldn't have asked."

"No, it's alright. I'm with a good man now and it sounds like George might have someone for him soon as well which will be good." May said with a tight smile and a sniff.

"We'll see. I've got to speak to Mac first."

With the bill paid they headed to the shops with May declaring, "I know a good place for an ice-cream later but first some retail therapy." She tucked her arm around Lily's again, "let's find something to tempt Georgie with." "You are terrible May." Lily laughed, "how are you so cheerful considering all you've been through?"

"I have friends and family who love me, a fiancée who worships me and a brother who adores me. What more does a girl need?" May laughed in turn, "I've always been told that I am like my great grandfather, hard to knock down. Georgie is more like our mother, the quieter type."

It was great to talk girlie nonsense all afternoon and try on clothes and buy a few as well. They ended the afternoon licking melting ice-cream cones on a bench looking out over the Menai Strait. Lily remarked, "thanks for inviting me out. Its been fun."

"Do you miss your London friends?"

"To be honest, not really. They come across frivolous now. Is it bad I want the 2.4 family now?"

"Not at all. Lives change. You own a farm now. You have responsibilities that they don't have." May remarked thoughtful, "you are a business owner really and you have an employee."

"True."

"Come on, shall we make a move? You coming with us to the National Sheepdog Trials?"

"Don't know. Have you been before?"

"Years a go. Georgie did manage to get through as a youth competitor. He's been determined ever since to get back. He's been training with Stan and Lou since they were pups. He didn't plan to have them as a pair but they worked well together. How's the training going with Bea?"

"Terrible. I'm wondering if I should leave it all to him." Lily answered as they walked back to May's car.

"That's cheating."

"He's so good at it though." Lily light-heartedly protested with a smile. Arriving back at the farm and as she walked into the hallway she called out, "George?" "In the kitchen."
She found him chopping vegetables for dinner. She hugged him, shopping bags and all, and kissed him on the cheek. With surprise he asked, "what was that for?"
"Your sister is amazing."
"I'm glad to you think so too." He replied with bemusement.
"I had a revelation with her help." She replied as she dumped the bags on the table.
He followed her through with a saucepan, "go on?"
"I've made a decision. I'm going to tell Mac it's over."
"Are you sure about that?"
"Yes." She said firmly, "I realised that I don't miss him as much as I should.
In fact I'm happy to be away from him and London."
"That's all right then."
She frowned, "aren't you happy about it?"
"You've got to do it first and let the dust settle."
"Don't you want to be with me?"
He took her by the shoulders, "I do but I also don't want you making any rash decisions. You've been with him a long time." She pouted.
"Don't sulk. You need to be sure you are doing the right thing. You had a big argument and all that has happened since is you've had a giant bunch of flowers. Have you actually spoken?"
"I haven't wanted to." She shrugged his hands off and headed upstairs grumbling. Why did he have to ruin what had been a good day? Why didn't he believe that she had really made her mind up? Men! One minute they were hot, the next cold. Why wasn't he happy that she had picked him? The underwear she had brought would have to wait.

Mac pushed his father's green Jaguar 1950s Roadster to go a little faster. This was a last ditched attempt to keep Lily. She hadn't responded to the huge bouquet he had sent so thought she was playing hard to get. He had a ring in his pocket ready to propose to her and a love-nest hotel room booked with champagne on ice for the celebrating. He would even move up to North Wales and commute if he had to but he would turn the outbuildings into more profitable holiday cottages. Then he would sell off most of the land but leave enough for Lily to play farmer with.

His phone rang and he grabbed it, "yeah....? Not at the moment... Ugh I hate country lanes." He squinted in the low light and pulled back into the middle of the narrow road once he had passed the quad bike with a scowl. He had left his sunglasses back in London and was regretting it, "yeah that sounds like a good deal, do it. No, no, don't worry about it..."

The road was slick from a brief heavy rain shower and the car slid briefly but he caught it in time and corrected. The dried dirt on the road had turned back to mud. He drove up the last hill and as he reached the brow the low sun half blinded him. He didn't see what was coming from the opposite direction till it was almost too late. At the last moment he saw a motorbike coming. Mac span the wheel but the car slid on the mud. There was a thud as the motorbike tried to swerve and went down. He swore as he finally came to a stop. He glanced out via the rear view mirror and couldn't see anything. Had he imagined it or had it been a stupid sheep? Whatever it was he couldn't see anything and he had other more important matters to attend to. He picked up his phone, "yeah, I'm fine. Think it was a sheep. Look, I'd best go as I'm nearly at Lily's... Thanks hopefully she will say yes."
He put the car back into gear and drove on.

George in a long sleeved t-shirt and jeans was on his way to the pub to meet up with his friends and May. It was too warm for his leathers and he was only going a short distance so was taking a risk. Considering the mud on the road he was going a bit slower then normal. Coming over the brow of the hill he found a Jaguar barrelling towards him in the middle of the road. He saw the driver look surprised.

The car tried to swerve but slid towards him. He tried to manoeuvre out of the way but he felt himself going over. He tried to lean away and right the bike but it was all happening too quickly. His right leg hit the corner of the car and his helmeted head bounced off the side as he crashed on to the road, jarring every bone in his body.

He fought the pain as he tried to keep control of the bike and turn the engine off. The bike had him pinned under it and dragged him off the road and down into a ditch as he managed to turn the key. It stopped, the wheels turning rubbing against the stonewall and causing the bike to hit his crotch. He winced and would have howled with pain if he could have. Tears well up. Once he had recovered enough he tried to move but the bike was too heavy on his leg and when he tried to raise up on his right arm he collapsed down with a moan of pain.

He heard the car stop and waited for the driver to come and help. He lifted his visor ready to talk to the idiot driver. Nothing. He heard the car drive off. He lay his head against the ground and fainted.

Davy glanced at his watch wondering where George had got to. He had rung to say he was on his way. May had gone for the first round of drinks. She was bringing them over on a tray when she felt weak at the knees. George's friends turned in horror as she they heard the sound of smashing glass. Davy rushed over to May who was on her knees holding her head, "are you all right?" She looked up, her pupils large, and whispered, "George."

Davy pulled out his phone and headed out of the pub while the barmaid helped May up and began to clean up the mess. Outside he found George's number and dialled with a shaking hand.

George felt his phone vibrate and came round. Slowly he moved his free arm to get it out of his trousers' back pocket. He saw Davy's name flash up and then become a missed call. He clung to his phone in hope his friend would try again. A minute later Davy rang again. He answered it on loud speaker and got Davy asking, "where are you?"

Through his helmet he said, "I'm in a ditch."

"I didn't hear you right. A ditch? Don't move Georgie, I'm coming." Davy didn't even bother to let the others know where he was going as he went straight for his car.

In the ditch George felt tears of relief welling up. He was glad someone now knew where he was. He didn't know which would have been worse- potentially dying at the hands of a sadistic thug or dying in a wet ditch because some moron had to make a phone call. At least Davy was on his way.

Fifteen minutes later Davy's headlight appeared and his car brakes squealed as they stopped. Davy called out, "Georgie?"

"Down here." George lifted his left arm.

Davy slid down the bank and found George trapped under his bike and his clothes torn, "Georgie! What happened? Hang on let me call an ambulance." He clambered back up the bank to make his phone call.

With it made Davy slid back down the bank, "all right, they are on the way. What happened?"

"Get the bike off. I can't feel my leg."

"All right, bear with me." Davy stood over his friend and with a grunt lifted the Triumph and with a wince let it fall away from him. George let out a loud moan as blood returned to his foot. Davy said, "I'm not going to move since you look in a bad way."

"Help me get my helmet off." George said. He reached for the buckle. Davy helped him out.

"It was some idiot on a phone in a Jag. He was going too fast for the road." George remarked with a groan as he shifted and Davy sat down beside him to wait for the ambulance.

The Jaguar limped into the yard. Mac got out to check the damage. His father would be fuming when he got back with the dented wing and door. He stomped across the yard grumbling at the barking dogs who ran out as Lily opened the front door. She looked surprised, "Mac? What are you doing here? Why didn't you ring?"

"I wanted to surprise you." He found a smile as he kissed her but frowned when she didn't reciprocate, "what's wrong?"

"Nothing. You've just surprised me."

"I'm here to take you away for a spur of the moment mid week break. Go pack."

"Mac, I can't."

"Why not?"

"George has gone out and we are going to the auction tomorrow."

"Why can't he go on his own? I thought you hired him for his knowledge." Mac snapped, "I've come all this way and probably hit a sheep and damaged my dad's car for you."

"You didn't have to." She pointed out while looking offended.

"Are you going to let me in?" He took a step forward and reluctantly Lily let him in. She didn't like Mac's attitude tonight.

"I think we should talk in the morning once you have calmed down." She remarked stiffly. She wasn't going to let him draw her into an argument. She wished George was there for moral support.

Before he could retort to that comment the phone rang. With relief Lily ran to answer it, "Hillside Farm?"

"Lily?"

Lily heard a tremble in May's voice and asked with concern, "May? What's wrong?"

"It's George. He was in a hit and run. Davy's with him in Bangor. Can you come and get me? I don't think I can drive there and get there in one piece."

"Where are you?"

"At the pub in the village."

"I'll be there as soon as I can." Lily answered, already searching for the Land Rover's keys, "is there anyone with you?"

"Moo and Bugsy but they lost their ride as Davy drove them over."

"Alright. Stay with them till I get there."

Mac demanded, "where are you going?"

She span round and glared at him, "a sheep? Did you really think it was a sheep?"

"They glow in the dark round here don't they?"

"That's the worse excuse I've ever heard." She snapped, "you hit my farm manager."

"Then he can pay for the damage." Mac declared feeling self satisfied that he now wouldn't have to pay for the damage.

"No he won't. Do you know I was going to do this tomorrow once we were both calmer but now..." She angrily shook her head. She felt Stan at her side and growl as if he could sense what was coming. She stood up straight, "Mac McGuire you are dumped."

"Dumped?!" He couldn't believe this was happening to him. He did it to women not the other way round. He

exclaimed, "I knew it! I just knew it! You are fucking him aren't you?!"
Lily put a hand on Stan's collar as his growl grew louder. Stiffly she said, "I think you'd best go."

"You slut." He shouted with one eye on the dog as the other two showed up behind Lily, "I hope you ruin yourself and then you'll wish you married me." He span on his heel and disappeared out the door.

Lily kept hold of Stan as she heard the Jaguar being over-revved and the gears crunch as Mac drove out of the yard. She took a deep breath as she sank to the floor. The dogs gathered round her and she hugged each one, "thank you doggies, now I need to go."

With her own gears crunching she made her way down to the village where May was waiting outside the pub with Moo and Bugsy. She gave them a wave as May climbed into the Land Rover. Moo called out, "let us know how
he is."

"Will do. Thanks boys, thanks Lily." May gave the other a tight smile.

"What happened May?" Lily glanced at her friend as she made her way to Bangor with May giving directions.

"Davy went and found him. He hasn't said much apart from the fact they went to Bangor. He's got some broken bones. I can't believe someone would just leave him there." May replied with fear. She pressed an imaginary accelerator pedal.

"I can." Lily remarked, "I think I know who it was."

"We have to tell the police. Who?"

"My now ex."

"Mac?!"

"He showed up at the farm wanting to take me to some hotel he booked claiming he'd hit a sheep on the way and I will tell the police but lets get to Bangor in one piece first."

Reaching the hospital they parked up and made their way to A&E. Davy was in reception waiting for them. He was relieved to see them and embraced May. He asked, "have you told your mum yet?"

"Not yet. I want to know how bad he is first. I don't want to scare her too much. Where is he?"

"X-ray to see how many broken bones he has and to check he hasn't done any damage to his kidney. He's got a bit of road burn as well. They said they'll come and get me when they bring him back."

"Is he okay?"

"He's awake and talking if that's what you want to know. They have drugged him up for the pain. The police are also waiting to talk to him."

"Where are they?" Lily asked, "I think I know who did it." Maybe she should have a sense of loyalty to Mac since they were together for so long but as he had abandoned the scene of the crime she didn't feel any compulsion to protect him.

They were sat with May between them when a nurse appeared. May gripped their hands tighter. The nurse said, "can you come with me." They all glanced at each other nervously as they stood and followed the nurse through the hospital. Realising where they were going May clung to Davy as she felt her legs loosing the ability to walk. Davy said to the nurse, "can we pause a moment."

May sank to the floor with Davy at her side. The nurse crouched beside her,

"are you okay? Take slow deep breaths."

"Tell us what is going on?" Davy requested.

"Are you family?"

"This is his sister and I'm his brother in law and best friend. I came in with him."

"He's in intensive care so he can be monitored. He has been sedated for the moment as he went into shock from the pain while we were investigating his injuries. Feel better?"

May nodded and carefully got up.

"He's not in danger. Ready?"

May nodded again and whispered, "thank you."

"The doctors are going to be able to tell you more."

The three of them sat round George's bed where his right arm was in plaster and sling. His shoulder was bandaged up. Under the blankets his thigh had a huge bruise on it as well as more bandage over his road rash. His calf and ankle was in plaster and they were monitoring his previously injured kidney. He slept heavily under the sedation.

May wanted to stay till George woke up but before long she was dozing.

She didn't really know why unless she was feeling what George was feeling.

Davy glanced over at Lily who nodded in agreement. It was time to go for now.

Davy said softly, "come on May, time to go home."

"I want to stay."

"He's not going anywhere and he's not in any danger and you are falling asleep on your feet."

"Come back to mine." Lily suggested.

"All right." May answered reluctantly. She leant over the bed and kissed her brother on the forehead, "I'll be back."

They got to the car park where May felt like she couldn't go any further. Davy swept her up into his arms and she wrapped her arms round his neck. She buried her face in his neck and with a sigh closed her eyes. Lily remarked as they found the Land Rover, "do you think she is feeling how George is?"

"Twins work in mysterious ways." He replied as he lay May on the back seat of the 4x4. As he climbed into the front seat he asked, "is it true that you've dumped Mac?"

"Yeah. He's an idiot. He claimed he thought it was a sheep."

"Arsehole." He muttered. Out of curiosity he asked, "are you going to get together with Georgie now?"

"How do you know?" She frowned.

"Who do you think?" He glanced behind at the sleeping May. Lily rolled her eyes. Well she never said to keep it a secret.

"I think you should get together with him."

"Maybe." She replied carefully, trying not to give anything away which was actually quite easy as she was concentrating on the road.

May didn't even stir as Davy carried her into the farmhouse and removed her clothes and put her to bed in one of the guest rooms. She woke in the morning trying to work out where she was. Her head felt woozy and then she remembered where they had been the previous night. She needed to go back. She scrabbled out of bed and shouted, "Lily?!"

"Downstairs." Lily called back.

May pulled her clothes on and ran down the stairs and declared, "we have to go back."

"Once you've eaten." Davy said from his seat at the table, "you slept like the dead last night. We think you were reacting to Georgie like you have before." He pushed a mug of tea towards his fiancee.

She sat down and took the tea gratefully. Her head still felt woozy. Maybe what Davy said was right. She had never felt so tried before and it certainly been a dreamless sleep. She suddenly realised she hadn't told her mother, "I need to tell Ma."

"Already done." Davy reassured her, "she's rung the hospital for an update and Georgie is still asleep. They're going to move him to a ward when he wakes."

15

It was afternoon visiting hours. May hurried through the corridors leaving Lily and her mother trailing behind. She almost jumped on her brother but restrained herself at the last minute. She exclaimed, "you need to stop doing this. Scaring us like this."

"Sorry." He winced as she carefully hugged him. From the carrier bag she was carrying she pulled out Bear, "look who I brought for you."

George tried to laugh but it just hurt too much, "thanks, very useful. No clothes then?"

"Lily has those."

He glanced over at Lily who smiled shyly at him and lifted the bag in her hand. She had had Hester's help in putting a pile of clothes, books and toiletries together for him.

"How are you feeling?" Hester asked as she gave her son a kiss.

"Like two separate halves." George tried to smile in jest, "I ache all the way down one side and I'm not going anywhere for a while. I don't think I'm going to the Sheepdog trials."

"Don't say that." May protested.

"Be realistic May. They are three weeks away. Even if I was on my feet with the aid of crutches I can't actually use them as I'm down to one free hand." He carefully moved his slinged arm.

May decided not to reply. She was sure she could come up with something. She allowed the conversation to flow over her.

It was Hester who realised that Lily and George kept glancing at each other. She touched May on the arm, "come on, let's get you home."

"I'm fine." May said distractedly.

"No, come on." Hester said more sternly and tried to discreetly gesture with her head at Lily. May realised then what was going unsaid and understood, "I'll see you tomorrow Georgie."

"I'd better otherwise I might go a wee bit insane." He joked.

George closed his eyes with a heavy sigh. Lily shifted nervously in her chair. Now they were as alone as they could get in a hospital ward she found she couldn't talk to him like they did on the farm. She even began to wonder if he had fallen asleep until he asked, "what happened at the farm?"

"What do you mean?"

"After he knocked me off the road."

"You know it was him?" She asked in disbelief.

"Yes."

"He thought you were a sheep."

"A sheep?" George asked in surprise and then tried to laugh, "he must be half blind to think I was a sheep. So, come on?"

"I dumped him."

He reached out with his left hand and she willingly took it in hers, "how does it feel?"

"Good. Relieved. He accused me of sleeping with you."

"Did you admit to it?"

"No. I'll admit to it now though." She smiled shyly.

"Cheeky and unfair as I can't act on that admittance." He winked and she giggled. Becoming serious he asked, "how did he react?"

"Not well. He got angry and threatened to send the bill to fix the car to you. Stan helped scare him off."

"Where do we stand now?"

"Where would you like us?"

"That's an unfair question." He protested, "I know what I would like though its a bit awkward at the moment."

"What is that?" She asked with a flirtatious smile. Did she dare kiss him or wait a bit?

"I think you know." He smiled.

"Now you are the cheeky one." She laughed.

"Lets do this properly. When I get out of here we'll go on a date. I'll come up with something." He so wanted to give her lips a kiss as she smiled at him. If only that prick Mac hadn't driven him off the road he would be taking her to bed right now. His hand became a fist in Lily's. She felt it and frowned, "is everything alright?"

"Just frustrated." He replied with a tight smile, "I'm sure Albert will help you if you ask."

"Your mother has already volunteered his services. I'm sorry you won't be able to go to the Sheepdog Trials."

"If I know May she'll come up with something."

Everyone came to visit when they could but he didn't enjoy being in hospital again. He ended up on sleeping pills to help him sleep through the pain and hospital noise. Mrs Rhys visited whenever she was on shift and was concerned for her son's best friend. He was definitely not one to be cooped up but there was nothing to be done about it. His visitors tried to keep up his moral with talk of everything from his bike being fixed and that Albert and Lily had sourced a tup for her.

Finally, after two weeks he was allow to go home though he still wasn't going anywhere fast. He hobbled slowly around on one crutch or sat in a chair in the house or garden or stayed in bed. It was good to be home although he wasn't going anywhere although he had heard that he was still in the sheepdog trials. He didn't know how May had done it but he was impressed not that he was sure how well it would go. There was a week to go and he couldn't do any training.

He didn't like relying so heavily on Lily but she was willing and his mother came over to help and feed them when she heard in horror it would be beans on toast until George was back on his feet. Mrs Rhys visited as well in her capacity as a nurse to help.

Hester found a small TV for George to have when he didn't feel like getting up. Lily left him dozing while she went to get them drinks. The dogs remained sprawled across the bed and claimed her spot. She heard knocking at the front door and opened it to find May and one of her friends at it. Lily asked cautiously, "May? What are you doing here?"

"We are here for an intervention."

"An intervention?"

"Yes. Davy is up the other end with Moo doing the same with Georgie." May grinned.

"Why do we need an intervention?" Lily stepped back to let May and her friend in.

"Because you two fancy each other and we are going to make it happen. Laura is here to make you irresistible. Come on, let's go and find a dress for you. Moo and I are sorting food and Davy is going to make George delightfully kissable." May said with excitement, "and then we are off to the trials tomorrow. This will give him the confidence he needs."

"May Rizoll you are so bad."

"And I love it." If she could have got away with it May would have skipped through the house.

A similar conversation was happening at the other end between Moo,
Davy and George. Davy declared, "we are going to get you all spruced up."

"Was this May's idea?"
Moo and Davy glanced between each other. George sighed. There was no way of stopping May when she got an idea in her head, "I don't know how successful this is going to be.

What's for dinner? It's not going to be very romantic if Lily is going to have to cut my food up."

"That's where I come in. I raided the frozen canapés. It's all finger food." Moo grinned.

George groaned, "are you really doing this Moo? You can't cook any more than Lily as I recall. You've boiled pasta dry before now."

"May is helping." Moo admitted, "I'm here for the grunt work."

"Do I dare ask?"

"You'll have to wait and see." Davy interrupted before Moo gave away all the surprises.

An hour and a half later and thankfully with no burnt food the stage was set in the garden. Moo had set up a table under a tree and had helped May arrange lanterns from the branches. Stepping back May was happy with the staging. She remarked to him, "lets do this. I'll get Lily if you can help Davy with Georgie."

Moo nodded, "see you in a bit. I don't know how long this will take."

Lily was led blindfolded into the garden by a giggling May. She was sat down and May said, "not yet."

"How long May?"

"Not yet."

"May, this is silly." Lily protested and reached for the blindfold but her hands were slapped away.

Fighting back the ache from his friends trying to help him with a few deep breaths George was helped outside by Davy and Moo. They got him round the corner of the house. Seeing the scene George remarked, "you have been busy." His eyes were staring at Lily.

Laura had done an amazing job of making Lily look stunning. Her brown hair had been brushed till it shone and a wave put into it. May had found in Lily's cupboard a white summer dress with large red poppies on it. A little mascara and plumish lipstick completed the picture.

"Well it is a bit hard to go on a date at the moment so it has been brought to you." Moo replied with a grin.

Over at the table May said to Lily, "now you can." With relief Lily pulled off the blindfold and gasped in surprise, "you didn't have to do all of this."

"Look over there." May pointed to where George was propped up by Moo. He was dressed in a t-shirt and shorts, all that would fit over his casts. Davy had removed the three week's worth of beard although he had caused a few cuts in his attempt to play barber. George smiled at her, "so you've been dragged into this as well."

"I'm not complaining." Lily blushed, "do you know what we are eating?"
George winced as Moo helped him into the chair, "it's not the most exciting. They cooked up some frozen canapes."

"This certainly won't be a date I'll be forgetting in a hurry." Lily laughed. Seeing the silly side of it George started laughing as well until his ribs caused him to stop.

"This isn't meant to be funny." May protested.

"Who wants food?" Laura appeared with two large plates of canapés.

"Look, why don't you all join us." George said, "I think you've all earnt it and there looks like there is quite a lot."

"But this is meant to be about you and Lily." May replied with a frown. Lily and George glanced at each other. George reached out for her and she took his good hand. She gave him a little nod and he looked back at his sister, "there is plenty of time for me and Lily to be alone. An evening in all your company would be just as good."

"Well I'm starving so I'm going to accept the invite." Moo interrupted as he heard his stomach growl, "budge up Lily." He sat on the bench next to her.
"Come on May." Davy looked at May.

"Oh alright." May sighed. Seeing that she was outnumbered, "come and join us Laura."

Laura grabbed some more chairs as May brought the last platter of canapés out.

Davy fetched the drinks.

After eating Moo and Laura excused themselves especially as Moo had the milking to do in the morning. Davy and May wandered off with their chairs and the leftover bottle of wine. The night was clear and May stared up at the stars. Davy saw her looking and remarked, "it's huge out there isn't it?"

"Davy?"

"Mmm?"

"I know we agreed on a long engagement but Georgie's accident, its sort of made me rethink. Life could be cut short at any time."

"He's going to be okay." He reassured her.

"I know. What I am badly saying is can we get married sooner?"

"You know I'll do whatever you want."

"You are too good for me."

He reached out and pulled her out of her chair and on to his lap, "no, I'm prefect for you." He buried his face in her neck. She giggled and turned her head so she could kiss him.

"Mmm, you are so yummy, I could eat you up." Davy murmured.

"Behave yourself." May gave him a playful slap.

"We could just go to bed?" He suggestively raised his eyebrows.

"You haven't answered my question yet." She protested.

"I would happily marry you tomorrow if I could but I would also wait five years if you asked me to." He kissed her, "let's go to bed."

"How about when George is well? I want him to walk me down the aisle."

"Hang on, I want him as my best man." Davy protested.

"We'll share him then."

"We have plenty of time to decide things May. Come on, lets go to bed." "All right."

Passing Lily and George they called out, "night." They grinned at each other when they realised Lily and George were engrossed in their conversation and didn't answer. Out of sight of the couple Davy and May high-fived each other before laughing.

When Davy and May left them Lily went for two blankets and George moved along the bench to be beside her. As Lily wrapped a blanket around him he remarked, "you know what they are up to don't you?"

"Oh yes."

"What should we do then?" He put an arm around Lily.

"Whatever we want to do. I'm ready to give it a go if you are." She glanced at his face which looked thoughtful. He looked up at the stars and remarked, "one year we brought each other stars. We like to imagine that they are both in the Gemini constellation. Silly aren't we?"

"That's sweet." She smiled.

"I'm up for giving it a go." He smiled his shy smile which she had grown to adore.

She loved the fact that he and May were yin and yang. He was so different to Mac as well. Whereas there were times that Mac put her on edge George left her calm and happy, happier then when she had been with Mac in a long time.

She cuddled up against George and he kissed her forehead. She smiled to herself. The evening would be even better if they could tumble into bed together but that would have to wait now. She would have to remain daydreaming of what George was like in bed. She giggled to herself. He frowned, "what is that for?"

"Nothing. What would we do for our first proper date?"

They spent a while coming up with fantasy dates and were so engrossed in competing for silliest, most romantic and the worst possible date that they didn't see

May and Davy head in. Their heads were close together and before long Lily's hands were holding George's face as they kissed.

With her kissing him he so wanted to sweep her into his arms. Damn Mac! He broke away and murmured while feeling loved up, "lets go to bed." "Mine or yours?" She whispered. She didn't want to disturb the mood.

"Yours is closer."

"I think Davy and May have already gone to bed." She looked round for them.

"Bear with me then." He smiled as he pushed himself up and reached for his crutch,

The dogs led the way up to Lily's bedroom. She helped George out of his shorts and with a giggle tucked him in. She hadn't drunk much but felt tipsy anyway. He couldn't help laughing sleepily at the silliness of it all. Any other time they would have been arousing each other until they could take no more. Instead, he was trying to hide his erection. Lily could feel it but so as not to embarrass him she didn't say anything as she snuggled up close to him.

Between two full land rovers everyone headed for the sheepdog trials on a farm near Abergavenny. One had Stan and Lou bouncing around in the back while the other was loaded with enough food and drink to feed an army. They were met by the Head Steward to discuss the plan to ensure that George would be able to participate within the rules. As he was only one of four braces competing it was all happening on day one.

It was agreed that he would go last with a steward driving him up. No words were spoken as he was driven up to the top of the field. He had no idea if this was going to work and wondered if he should just forfeit and try again next year but he couldn't let his friends and family down at the last minute.

He slowly and carefully got out and paused, resting on his crutch, and heard the polite applause coming from the bottom of the field. He looked round, taking in the lay of the land. There was a dip in the field. He stood on one edge of it by the post while the flock of eight sheep were in the sloping top corner of the field. The two gates marked with fencing ran from left to right diagonally on either side of the dip. The shedding circle was at the bottom of the dip where there was also the pen. He was glad there were no awkward spots where he could lose sight of the sheep and dogs so he didn't have to hobble round too much.

The steward in his bib came round and smiled encouragingly, "ready?"

"The best I will be. Can you let them out?"

"Sure."

As Stan and Lou jumped out George called them to heel and they ran to where he stood by the post. They sat at his feet, eyes on the small flock.

"In your own time."

George nodded, pulled out his dog whistle and took a deep breath to calm his nerves. It would be nice to win but he had seen the competition. He would settle for third.

With a command he sent Stan and Lou off to round up the small flock and then drive them up behind him and round. They drove them pass him and then down through the two sets of gates to the marked shedding circle. He held the sheep there with his two collies while he and the steward slowly headed down. As he came to the circle the steward continued down to the pen. He split two of the flock away with the dogs before uniting them back and then drove them across to the pen which the steward closed on the hesitant sheep once they were in. The flock resisted at first and he had to circle the sheep round and try again.

With the gate re-opened Stan and Lou drove the flock back out and back to the shedding circle. Now came the difficult bit, getting one of the collared sheep out without the rest following or dispersing. He ordered the panting dogs to lie down while he tried to calm his beating heart. He took a nervous gulp before ordering Lou to stay where she was and then sending Stan off into the flock.

Frustratingly the two collared sheep were in the centre so he struggled to drive them to the edge without all of them crossing the white line. With stop starts they reached the edge and then one trotted over the line. He didn't realise he was holding his breath between whistles until he let out a long sigh as he heard applause. He looked up and grinned with relief and raised his hand in acknowledgement as the steward went for the Freelander. He had done the best he could and now could only wait.

He came in a well deserved third.

16

A few weeks later everyone was at the pub to celebrate the removal of George's casts. As he walked in with a limp and Lily's hand in his a cheer rose from his and May's friends. Lily blushed. Bugsy exclaimed, "finally. How long have you been hiding this?"

It was George's turn to blush, "not that long. We are giving it a go that's all."

May and Davy looked knowingly at each other.

"Are you going to keep him out of hospital now Lily?" Moo asked.

"I'll do my best." Lily laughed as they joined the group. Under the table she squeezed George's hand.

"Has the money come through yet?" Bugsy asked.

"The other day. I even got a phone call from his father." George answered.

"His father is a really nice man." Lily added, "I think he would be rather embarrassed that Mac caused such an avoidable accident. Mac on the other hand would have got a bollocking."

Annoyingly there hadn't been enough evidence to prove it had been Mac who had hit him and then abandoned him on the side of the road.

Davy laughed at the thought, "good, because if he had shown his face up here again. I think he would have been backed into a corner if you get my drift."

"It's all right he won't be coming up here."

"Going out on your bike soon?" Davy turned to George as Lily's attention was pulled away by May's friends who were all now feeling a little jealous that the new girl had caught George's attention.

"As soon as I get a moment. I just need to sort out the farm first. Thanks for looking after it."

"I wouldn't think of doing anything else. May and I have something to tell you."

"Mmm?" George looked suspiciously at his best friend over his pint as he took a large sip from it.

"We are going to get married a lot sooner then planned. Your accident made her realised how important it was not to waste a day. The problem now is we both want you." George chuckled, "you'll have to share me then."

May interrupted, "what are you going to spend the money on?"

"I might get some Balwens if Lily will let me. The rest I'll keep safe."

"Lily, did you hear that?"

Lily turned, "hear what?"

"Can George get some Balwens?"

Lily looked at George and with a smile replied, "of course he can."

"Yeah." May hugged Lily.

Davy and George laughed and then George remarked, "it's good to be out."

"Everything is looking bright." Davy added and they chinked their pint glasses.

"I agree."

Spotting what the best friends had done Moo said loudly, "a toast?" He raised his glass and once everyone else had raised theirs he went on, "to survival."

"That's a bit morbid." Bugsy frowned.

"Well what would you say then?" Moo protested.

"To many more bright days ahead." Davy grinned.

"Bright days." Everyone replied and took a drink before returning to their interrupted conversations.

It was a good night and everyone was enjoying themselves and reluctantly parted when the last orders bell was rung. There were groans which the barmaid cheerfully reacted to, "we all have homes to go to."

"Spoilsport." Davy called out.

The barmaid stuck her tongue out at them, ignoring the fact she was in her fifties. They all laughed and then finished their drinks off.

Outside there were hugs and plans made for the near future. They waved to each other as they headed their separate ways. George and Lily climbed into the Land Rover. As Lily started the engine she asked, "why do they like the fact we are together?"

"Who knows, but their opinions don't matter do they?" He replied, "they didn't bring us together."

"They tried." She laughed.

"That is true. I do know May is keen to see me settled with someone and she has decided on you for the moment. It could have been anyone. I've broken some hearts in the past when I've gone out with someone."

"I think you've done it again tonight. Some of May's friends were giving me evil looks."

George chuckled, "don't mind them."

They hesitated at the farmhouse door. Since May's date night they hadn't been together in bed. There had been some kissing but not much more. Just this morning George had crept up on her in the kitchen now that he had finally been freed from his casts; and swept her up into his arms and kissed her quite passionately. If only they hadn't had B&B guests she probably would have let him take her there and then.

It was all a bit novel. It had been a long time since she and Mac had been young fresh loves eager to kiss and touch each other. At the moment she could never grow tired of it.

As George turned to head to his own bed she grabbed his arm. He raised an eyebrow, "are you sure?"

She shyly smiled and nodded and drew him through the back door. He let her draw him upstairs whereupon he couldn't wait any longer. He stepped ahead and pulled her through her bedroom door. He dropped on to her bed and pulled her on to his lap. She giggled until his kiss silenced her. She wrapped her arms around his neck as his hands moved up her back, under her shirt, and found her bra. She pushed him back on to the bed. He watched as she pulled her shirt off and then her bra. She wiggled out of her jeans and knickers and hoped the queasiness would stay away long enough for her to enjoy the sex that was clearing coming. She watched as he shrugged off his own clothes while remaining lying on the bed.

They froze then as neither had really been purposely naked before each other. They didn't count the moment in the bathroom. He lay still as she sat on him. She ran her hand over his chest and then her finger over his face, teasing him. He snapped at her finger as she let it run over his lips. She giggled and then bent over him to kiss his lips. He grabbed her hips and she gasped as he guided her on to his erection. She carefully rode him until they both came.

She slept wrapped in his arms. Waking in the morning she didn't want to get up and spoil anything. She snuggled into the space where George was and discovered him gone.

She smiled with relief when he reappeared in jeans and bare feet and carrying a tray of breakfast. He knew she wouldn't care about his operation scar. His black hair was all messed up. He was too handsome and he was all hers. He grinned as she looked blurredly at him, "morning. Breakfast in bed?"

"That sounds lovely."

"Excellent. Make space then." He placed the tray between them and got back on the bed, "now, pretty lady, what are you doing in my bed?"
She pushed him, "don't be silly."

"Sorry, it's not that exciting. Toast and tea."

"That's fine with me. Can we stay in bed all day?" She asked wistfully.

"You can if you want. I've got the farm to sort out and all those sheep Albert helped you buy. You've doubled the size of the flock."

"He said they were all good." She blushed.

"You might make a little money next year and you are going to learn to milk if you want to make cheese."

"Yes sir." She saluted him and giggled.
He rolled his eyes as he reached for his mug of tea.

She slyly studied him as they ate the cooling toast smothered in melted butter. He sat back leaning against the headboard occasionally rolling his shoulder to ease the stiffness. Did she dare reveal her secret now? The longer she waited the worst it would be when George found out but she didn't want to spoil the moment either.

Her body made the decision as she found herself running to her small ensuite. She didn't like the morning sickness although it lingered all day and she wondered why it was even called morning sickness. Some days it had been easier to hide how she was feeling but clearly not today. George followed behind a few minutes later when he realised something was wrong. He cautiously knocked on the door on the door, "are you alright?"

"It's not locked."
Slowly he opened the door to find Lily sat on the floor by the toilet. He wasn't sure how to react when he saw her brush tears from her cheek, "Lily? What's wrong?"

"I don't know how to tell you." She really didn't. She wanted to enjoy the early lust filled moments and instead she was sat by the toilet.

"Tell me what?" He reached for her towel robe from behind the door and handed it to her.

She sniffed and pulled it on.

He crouched down beside her and his ankle protested, "tell me what?"

"I'm pregnant."

"Oh." He sat down on the floor by her side on. He didn't know what to say to that surprise.

"I haven't wanted to ruin our moments together but…."

"Is it Mac's?"

She shook her head, "that last time we didn't have any sex."

"Oh."

The silence sat between them. Her head hung low as George tried to come to terms with it, "we've only had sex once… Aren't you on the pill or something?"

She shook her head, "they gave me headaches and nausea. Mac and I used condoms."

"Oh."

"Say something different then that." She pleaded.

"I never thought I would say this but I need to think about this." He stood and walked out of the bathroom leaving Lily staring wide eyed at his bare back. Had he really just said that?! She wanted to scream and stamp her feet and demand he come back and face his responsibilities. Instead she found herself heaving into the toilet bowl again; the stress too much.

George pulled on clean clothes, found his phone and grabbed his helmet and bike keys. The dogs pranced around him but he shooed them away as he mounted his bike. He took a deep breath as he turned the key in the ignition. He had a brief sense of trepidation of getting back on his bike. Anything could happen as shown by Mac. He told himself not to be foolish and set off. He needed to ride, clear his mind and make a decision.

He rode round the country lanes until he came into the village and to Rhys' Garage. He pulled up outside.

Davy was inside working on a car, foot tapping to the music on the radio. He knew then he wanted his best friend's advice. He walked in.

Sensing a presence behind him Davy turned and was surprised to find George standing just inside, helmet in hand, "Georgie? What are you doing here? You all right, you look a bit pale."

"I'm not sure. You got a minute?"

"Mmm. Sure. Come on, we'll go next door." Davy abandoned the car and led his friend into his parents' kitchen. He put the kettle on and found the biscuit tin. His mother entered, "do I hear the kettle and biscuit tin? Oh, hello George. How are you doing? Glad to be out of the casts?"

"I am, thank you Mrs Rhys." George replied from the kitchen table, "I'm just waiting for an appointment to check all the bones are okay now the casts and slings are gone."

"Ma." Davy protested, "you aren't at the hospital."

"Trying to have a man-to-man conversation are you?" She teased.

"Ma!"

"All right, all right, I'm going." She held her hands up in mock defence. She left, shutting the door behind her.

With her gone Davy raided the biscuit tin, "go on George, what's wrong?"

George shifted in the chair, "do you remember the day that Mac tried to provoke us?"

"That shit bag. What about it?"

George sipped his tea, "well… me and Lily ended up..."

Davy broke into the biggest grin George had ever seen, "oh you… that is hilarious." He had never known George to be impulsive. His face dropped when he realised George wasn't laughing with him, "oh…?"

Yeap." George said into his mug and his shoulders relaxed with relief that Davy understood what he was badly trying to say. The word didn't need to be said as they were that in tune with each other.

"Is she sure?"

"They didn't have any sex that weekend. Davy, what the hell do I do?" He put his head in his hands, "my first instinct was to propose to her."

"That's a bit noble and drastic isn't it?"

"What else can I do? I am such an idiot."

"At least don't fall on your sword just yet. She didn't stop you so she wanted it as much as you; but you are a jammy dodger keeping that quiet. The pair of you need to talk."

"Don't tell May, please." George pleaded.

"I won't tell her. You know I won't."
As if he had only just realised George rubbed a hand over his face, "I'm going to be a dad."

"And I get to be the fun uncle then. Does she want to keep it then?"

"I don't know." George finished his tea and stood, "I'd best go. She's probably freaking out."

"Good luck. Let me know what happens. You know May and I have your back." He gave his best friend a hug of encouragement.

"Thanks."

Still not really sure how to deal with it all George returned to the farm where Lily was chewing on a nail at the dining table. She stood up looking afraid.

"I just needed to clear my mind."

"I didn't want it to come out how it did."

"The fact you are still pregnant means I guessing you want to keep it?" He said from the doorway.

"Come and sit down." She pleaded, "and I suppose I do."

"What do you want from me?" He came and sat down opposite her.

"You don't have to marry me." She laughed stiffly. She saw his shoulders relax. She went on, "this is modern times. We don't have to marry. We've only just become a couple so shall we play it by ear? We pretty much live in the same house so he or she will have both parents to hand."

George smiled, "sounds like a plan." He stretched out a hand across the table and she put hers in his. He gave it a squeeze, "I'm going to be a father."

"Yes, and I'm sorry."

"It's much my fault as yours. We created it together."

"We did." She smiled, "do you want to come with me when I go for the first scan?"

"That would be nice. Right," he stood, "I need to go and check on all these ewes and the tup you've brought. Coming?"

"Yes."

In an uncomfortable silence they walked up the fields to where Lily's flock were nibbling at the grass. The dogs ran ahead and began herding the sheep together. Lily laughed, "I don't think we are going to get away from doing any work."

"I'll get them down into the next field and then see how they look. Do you want to go and open the pen and we'll get them in there."

"Sure." She walked down as he whistled to the dogs. Stan and Lou's ears pricked up and he sent them to left and right while he kept Bea at his side. He knew he was going to need to do some proper training with her as Lily had given up her half hearted attempts. Bea whined, wanting to be out with her parents. He put down a hand and rubbed the young collie's head.

With the sheep in the holding pen he let them out slowly, looking for lameness or any other issues. Though he wanted to grab them and give them a thorough check he knew his shoulder wasn't up to the task yet. He would have to trust his brother's judgement for the moment. As the last one filtered out Lily asked, "well? How do they look?"

"Not bad. Lets go look at the tup. Where is he?"

"In one of the smaller fields. Albert said to keep him separate so he's sharing a field with the ponies."

"Lead the way."

The ram appeared to glare at them as the dogs cornered it while the ponies looked on. If they could create such an expression they would have looked bemused. It tried to head-butt George as he approached but he grabbed the ram by its horns. It struggled as he stepped over it to hold the ram still by his thighs. He checked the ram's teeth and testicles. All looked good. Satisfied he let the ram go. With a shake of its horned head it trotted away. Lily asked, "well?"

"He found a good one. I'm surprised he didn't take it for himself."

"He did hint he might like to borrow it."

"I think that would be fair." He replied as he held out a hand. She glanced at it. Was this a peace offering? She decided to take it. He smiled and brought her hand to his lips, "mummy."

"Ssh." She smiled and blushed but didn't pull her hand away.

The ice had been broken and they returned to their normal relaxed conversation and banter. They found themselves coming up with baby names that rapidly became a competition for the silliest. Concentrating for a moment George came up with his next suggestion, "Tarquin?"

"Tootsie?"

George chuckled, "ok, yours is sillier. Mine just sounds pretentious."

She giggled and then said, "I'm running out of ideas now."

"So am I. Shall I make us some lunch?"

"Oh that reminds me?"

He eyed her suspiciously as he raided the fridge and remarked, "we need to go shopping."

"My parents are coming this weekend. Any chance you can make dinner?" She peered round the fridge door and attempted to flutter her eyes.

He rolled his as he closed the door, "when were you going to tell me?" She blushed.

"What do you want cooked?"

"They don't like fancy food, no spice."

"I'll think about it. You really are going to have to learn to cook more than a fried breakfast."

"But I've got you." She hugged him.

"Suck up."

"Thank you." She grinned, "oh and can I sleep in your bed? We have a full house so they'll have my room." George sighed, "fine."

She kissed him on the cheek.

17

Though they had heard about everything going on this was the first time they had visited. Lily's mother helped her make up the rooms while the guests were out, "are you enjoying it all?"

"I am. I've recently brought some more ewes."

"You said. How is your farmhand? Aren't you worried about his fitness if he has been in hospital twice in the last year." She had only been told a little by Lily about what had gone on.

"He's fine mum. He's just had bad luck."

"When do we get to meet him?" She eyed her daughter over the pillow she was plumping.

"He's out in the yard somewhere I think but he's making dinner."

Her mother sighed, "I tried so hard but you could never cook and then you and
Mac..."

"I don't want to talk about him mum."

"Why ever not?"

"You know why not. It ended badly but I'm glad to be rid of him."

"Have you no good memories?"

"Yes but I've moved on. He didn't want me here and I want to be here." She reminded her mother.

"Are you seeing anyone now?"

"Sort of." Lily blushed. As they moved on to the last room she went on,
"mum, I have a confession."

"Oh?" Her mother looked worried.

"I'm pregnant."

"Oh? Is it Mac's?"

"No." Lily distracted herself with the pillows.

"Whose is it then?" Her mother frowned.

"It's George's."

"Oh."

"Mum. Can you stop saying oh."

"What else can I say?" Her mother stared at her daughter, "you are pregnant by a man you say you've only just started dating. Are you sure its not all lust from living in close proximity?" "Mum!" Lily protested.

"What? I don't want to think you are being taken advantage of."

"I'm not."

"Mmm." Her mother would make a final decision when she met this Welshman.

Lily's father was wandering the farm buildings, having a nosy in them. He found George sitting on the ground tinkering with his bike. George glanced up, "hello? You must be Mr Harrison? I would shake your hand but mine's a bit oily."

"Don't worry about that." Robert Harrison replied, "you must be George?"

"I am."

"What are you up to?" The elder man crouched down at George's side.

"Just fixing the bike. Think there's a loose part somewhere." He let the older man have a quick glance. Looking at the man he couldn't really see Lily in him. He came across quite practical as Robert pushed his glasses on to his forehead to study the bike's parts a bit closer.

The two men found themselves hitting it off. They spent two hours together finding the fault and fixing it. By the end Robert Harrison was impressed by the younger man. He definitely preferred him to Lily's old boyfriend who looked down at him and his wife, "can handle sheep and fix an engine?"

"My friend Davy is better at the engine bit then me."

"And good tastes with the Triumph. I always fancied one."

"Davy and I put it back together."

"You ride?"

"Yes. You?"

"Once, a long time ago." Robert sighed. He was impressed at how well George was recovering from his motorbike accident. He suggested, "I think it's time for a cuppa. What do you think?"

"I've got dinner to make."

"Lily still can't cook then. She takes after me on that. I easily burn toast." Robert grinned.

"I've had to put up with beans on toast before now. Thanks for your help."

"It was fun."

Amanda Harrison eyed George suspiciously as he moved around the kitchen, trying to work him out. She felt sure he was too good to be true. Her husband was already singing his praises. She could see why Lily was attracted to him as he was definitely handsome. After dinner she decided that Lily should keep him and never let him go. She asked, "where did you learn to cook like that?"

"My mother and grandfather." He replied as he cleared the table.

"How about a walk?" Lily interrupted before her mother could ask any more questions.

"I would be happy with a nap. I'm stuffed." Robert announced.

"A walk sounds nice." Amanda remarked and sternly eyed her husband who backed down under the look, "you could show us all the land you own." "We'll go to the top of the hill." Lily suggested, "coming George?"

"I've nothing else planned."

"Excellent." Robert exclaimed, "it will be good to have some male company."

While the men walked ahead with the dogs the two women walked arm in arm. Lily remarked, "now you have met him, what do you think?"

"I'll let you off. He seems to be a good man. The important thing is that you are happy."

"I am." Lily leant into her mother, "I didn't realise that I had fallen out of love with Mac till I was up here. We had fallen into a too comfortable routine."

"Don't you have that here as well?" Her mother challenged.

"But this feels more normal, more real." Lily insisted, "Mac and I lived in a fantasy land. We spent money to be happy. I feel happier here."

"I don't want to see you get hurt that's all."

"I'm a big girl mum." Lily protested, "can we talk about something else now"

"All right. What do you want to talk about then?"

"Anything. How are you and dad?"

"We miss you since you are all the way up here." She hugged her daughter, "I think the boys are waiting for us."

The rest of the afternoon and evening went well. Robert joined George as he fed the animals, enjoying himself more then he thought he would. He felt like a child as he helped shut the chickens and ducks in. He knew it was all a lot harder work then most people thought so was glad his daughter had quickly sourced knowledgeable help. George seemed to know what he was doing as he walked round with his slight limp. He told his wife so when they retired to Lily's bedroom for the night.

In the morning George left Lily in his bed and went to make the guests' breakfasts. This was where Amanda found him and was a little surprised. She had hoped to find her daughter in the kitchen and be impressed that she could at least cook up a cooked breakfast, "oh, I thought Lily did this?"

"Normally. I've let her lie in bed. Want a cup of tea?"

"Please."

She drank her tea as George prepared breakfast for the five guests who were sat round the table in the dining room. As he plated up she asked, "is she alright here?"

He glanced at Lily's mother and realised the way she frowned was similar to

how Lily frowned. He asked back, "What do you mean?"

"Everything. However much you think your children confide in you there are also things that get left unsaid."

"You don't go into farming to get rich quick. This year is only the first and will leave her in the red." George replied honestly, "next year will be better as now the flock is double its size. She'll have more lambs to sell or keep. She has a tup she can rent out if she wants. The B&B side can only really grow. And she has surprised me with her cheese making. Her biggest expenses are me and the business loan she has. Is that what you wanted to know?"

"Thank you for your honesty." Amanda said as she helped George carry the plates through, "don't tell her I asked."

"I won't."

"You are a good man."

George blushed, "I am just doing my job apart from this and making sure we eat more than beans on toast."

Amanda laughed, "she never could cook."

"She tries. She tried to bake a cake once and got flour everywhere." George laughed, "my first meal from her was a burnt chilli. Right, our turn, what do you fancy for breakfast?"

18

A few weeks later George and Lily had his family round to tell them of the exciting news with the pictures from the scan which had revealed two foetuses. Though Hester did also tell them off for being so foolish causing George to blush and Davy to laugh as he knew how and when it had happened.

After everyone had recovered from the surprise apart from Davy and had congratulated George and Lily and asked whether they knew the sexes, May cleared her throat. George looked over, "May?"

"I, well we, have something to say as well."

"What?"

"Davy and I have booked ourselves in the registry office in November."

Even Hester was surprised at that as May hadn't said anything to her. Davy looked embarrassed as George looked disappointed. He wished he had known May was going to say something as he would have stopped her. This was not the time to be competing with her twin, this was a time for George and Lily to have the family limelight. As May opened her mouth Davy put a hand on her arm and shook his head when she looked at him. Reluctantly May took the hint and closed her mouth. Already she was beginning to realise her mistake.

The group around the table relaxed and returned to talking about George and Lily's plans. George gave his sister a grateful smile and she nodded in understanding. This time it was his turn to be happy especially now he had seen the growing babies.

Lily and himself have become a tighter unit since she had revealed the pregnancy. Their desire for each other hadn't diminished and now George's family knew they felt they could truly start preparing for the arrival of the babies and they becoming a family.

As they got ready to leave George and Davy stepped off to one side. They embraced as George said, "thanks for stopping May."

"You hide behind her sometimes and this time it was your turn to stand in front." Davey remarked, "And I think she just wants to tell everyone. It was only confirmed today."

"I'm happy for you. So, am I best man or giving her away?"

"We tossed a coin actually." Davy laughed.

"And who won?"

"Me." Davy grinned.

"So what date is it and I'll make sure we are there. Is there going to be a party?"

"November 14th. It's a friday. We're going to have the village hall. We don't have a lot of money." Davy blushed.

"Family is what matters. Welcome to the family." George grinned, putting his friend at ease.

"What about you and Lily? Got over that urge to propose?" Davy teased

"We are happy as we are. We've got plenty of time." May approached, "you coming Davy?"

"Coming." He gave his friend another hug, "see you later daddy."

George laughed, "you too uncle." He followed them to the cars and stood beside Lily.

He put an arm round Lily as they waved the two cars off. As they disappeared they headed back in and Lily asked, "you and Davy okay?"

"Yeah, we're good. Sorry about May throwing that in tonight. Davy said they only got the appointment confirmed today."

"It's all right. When is it happening?"

"November 14th. I'll do the dishwasher in the morning. Let's head to bed."

The CD player was on and everyone was having fun as Davy and May's friends decorated the village hall. At least a mile of paper chains had been created and hung from the ceiling. The tables and chairs were arranged and covered in paper tablecloths. The place settings were laid and then their work was done for the evening so they retired to the pub. Come the next day there would be some proper celebrating.

The next day in the registry office George kept Davy company, both of them wearing new dark grey suits with white shirts and grey ties, while behind them Lily sat, one of the first in the room. She felt the babies kicking and smiled. One was being on the lively side at that moment. Seeing her smile George asked, "okay?"

"One of them is moving again. I think he's excited for his uncle." Davy gave her a nervous smile.

"Everything's going to be all right." George reassured his best friend. "I know. It's just standing here and wondering if she will show up." Davy replied as the guests filtered into the room.

"She will." George put a hand on Davy's shoulder as the guests started to filter in, "not long now."

The registrar walked down the aisle and set himself up with his assistant. Then the traditional wedding march started and everyone turned to the door. May stepped through at Albert's side, her hair wavy and woven through with red rosebuds. She wore a long red evening gown for her wedding dress that Lily had helped her choose. It had a low back with the ends of a sash trailing behind her. Her tanned skin shone and her red lips beamed at the sight of Davy in his dark grey suit tugging at his collar. In her hands she had a small bouquet of red roses.

George met them halfway down the short aisle. He took her from Albert who smiled at his brother. He led May the rest of the way and put her hand in Davy's. A compromise had been worked out.

There was clapping and cheers as the new Mr and Mrs Rhys were presented by the registrar and the pair blushed. Their exit piece started playing, 'Celebration', and the newly married couple led the way from the registry office and were seen off before everyone were reunited at the village hall.

The party went late into the night though various guests came and went as dictated by the life of a farmer. George and Lily slipped away halfway through the night with May and Davy's blessing. George drove them home, "a good night?"

"Definitely but I'll be glad to see our bed."

"I've been thinking about this for a while and don't want to admit it but Mac was right on one thing?"

"Where is this going?" She asked suspiciously.

"Well… since my end isn't really used any more why don't we do it up as a self-catering cottage especially as at some point we will be losing a guest room for a nursery and maybe do some of the outbuildings. We should probably create you a proper little dairy for your cheese."

"Mmm." Lily was falling asleep.

George chuckled to himself, "okay, we'll talk in the morning."

Epilogue

Before anyone knew it Christmas had arrived. After making sure the animals at Hillside Farm had enough for the day George and Lily drove over to the family farm so he could help his mother in the kitchen. The dogs joined the others alternating between begging for food and lying in front of the fire with Lily on the sofa growing larger with the twins. Albert's two children ran around and called out when May and Davy arrived with his parents. There were more cheerful call outs and hugs. May rolled up her sleeves, "what can I do to help? How's the renovation going?"

"We'll be done in time for the new season. It finally has a kitchen." George smiled as he handed a bowl of sprouts over for May to trim, "excited for the new job?"

"And scared." May admitted.

"It's only Wrexham so you can still visit." Hester pointed out, "or I can come and see you with George."

"Don't worry we will be visiting since I'll have my nephews to see." She grinned over at George who didn't see it as his back was to her now, "but it's just the furthest we've ever been which feels mad." May admitted at the end as she sat at the scrubbed kitchen table to trim the sprouts.

"Victoria?! Can you get the table laid?" Hester called out.

"Ok grandma." The girl answered and came to get the cutlery.

They all sat at the table pulling crackers as Albert carved the ham and George the leg of lamb. Who needed a turkey when you could have a piece of lamb from the family's flock. Everyone else passed round the vegetables.

With everyone's plates full Albert stood, "I think we need a toast."

He shuffled when he realised all their eyes were on him. He cleared his throat, "it has certainly been an interesting year. We can celebrate the return of our sister." He glanced at May who blushed, "we can celebrate the return of George's good health. We can also welcome new members to the family. So a toast to a better year." He raised his pint. Everyone else raised their glass. Under the table George and Lily held their free hands. George glanced across the table and smiled his soft smile at May and Davy. Davy grinned back. Hester gazed round at her family, content that it was complete again and growing. If only her husband was here to see it. She raised her glass the highest, "to a happy new year."

About the Author:

I am an independent author, writing since my teens. I don't have the money or the weight of a publishing house behind me so every sale and every review is truly appreciated.

Please follow me on Instagram @f_garstang_author for more about me and the books I have self published or are working on.

Fanny Garstang